TELEPHONE TALES

BY

MICHAEL WENNER

This book is a work of fiction. Places, events, and situations in this story are purely fictional. Any resemblance to actual persons, living or dead, is coincidental.

First published by AuthorHouse 05/06/04

ISBN: 1-4184-0686-4 (e-book)
ISBN: 1-4184-0687-2 (Paperback)
ISBN: 1-4184-0688-0 (Dust Jacket)

This book is printed on acid free paper.

To The Narrator

These stories are written mainly, though not

exclusively, for children. Like most such tales, they are

designed to be read aloud and they have proved very

popular with many young audiences. The stories are

moreover short enough to offer entertainment within the

brief span of a two to three minute telephone call and they

have in fact been successfully told long-distance at bedtime

over the phone. The more expressively and colorfully they

are read, the more they are enjoyed. So, narrators, come out strongly with your sheep bleats, pooch growls, dragon snorts, a good 'yi-ucks' at the smell of garbage, and all the other important sound effects suggested in the texts; and have fun narrating as you go!

Some of the Tales may contain words new to young audiences. - ('Grandma - what does 'dawdle' mean, and what is a 'shrew'?) — So a glossary is provided [at P ix to xiv] for you to consult if necessary. The stories can in this way usefully serve as effective vocabulary expanders, without taking substantially longer to read.

A few illustrations are provided for audiences being read to direct. Listeners may, however, like to draw their own interpretations of, say, Holy MacRoary, Busybody Sniff or Dog Molecule. In our own family, Captain

Trumpet and Aunt Crotchety have proved popular subjects for grandsons to Fax back to Grandad.

A pleasant surprise has been that despite or perhaps because of the quirky nature of these stories, they have been shown to appeal to parents with a sense of humor as well as to offspring.

Read on!

Characters

Geordie - an ordinarily nice young lad

Suzie - his little sister, known as 'Mim' when she was very

    small.

Mom & Dad - his parents

dog Molecule - Geordie's dog

Aunt Crotchety - Mom's unmarried sister, who lives with

    Geordie & Suzy.

Moggins - Aunt Crotchety's cat

Granpa Thrush - Mom's Dad

Uncle Pickle - rancher

Josh - Uncle Pickle's ranch foreman

Molly - a friend of Suzy's

Great granny Periwinkle - Dad's gran

Miss Scratchit - Geordie's & Suzy's school teacher

Miss Stringit - Suzy's music teacher

Willie Jim - a young country lad

Captain Trumpet - local police chief

Jim - the Mailman

Old Miss Trundle - a sharpish neighbor

Aunt Daisy & Great uncle Hank - Dad's relatives

Poor Old Gertrude - a handicapped lady who lives in the
    subdivision

Gregory - Geordie's classmate

Zoltan Fracas - another classmate

Farmer Growler - owner of fine dairy cows

Woops - one of his finest dairy cows

Doris - a young maid

Holey MacRoary - Troll

William the Worm - garden resident

doña Pancha - a peccary wild pig

Shem, Ham & Japhet - green lizards

Big Snorter - Dragon

Rumbold - Dragon & Clockabill

Sniff - Busybody & Witch

Gwendoline - dog Molecule's Poodle friend

Sizzler Sockit - a rock star

Glossary - some quick answers in case of emergency, and to help you get to know some new and useful words.

Telephone Tales I

TT I - 1   -'shrew' - a tiny, savage, mouse-like creature

-'pack-horse' - a horse once used to carry loads, sometimes heavy ones

-'mackintosh' - a long raincoat, useful in rainy countries.

TT I - 3   -'recall' - to 'call back', or 'remember'

TT I - 4   -'confided to' - 'told privately'

TT I - 5   -'measly' - 'tacky', 'crummy', 'yucky'

TT I - 6   -'the adjoining field' - 'the field next door'

TT I - 7   -'City Councilman' - one of the prosperous-

looking top people who run your City

-'jowls' - floppy, loose flesh each side of the jaw

TT I -9   -'wrath and doom impending' - an old English

hymn title, meaning 'the approaching end of the

world' (doom), when God's anger (wrath) will be

threatening people who've been bad

TT I -10   -'straying'- 'wandering off'.

-'glazed over' – 'fixed and glassy'

-'Gladstone Bag' - a stiff leather bag with handles

on top

TT I -11   -'a scuffling noise' - noise of heavy shuffling of

feet

TT I -11   -'native habitat' - where they were born

TT I -12 -'porcelain' - what the very best dinner plates are

made of

-'greengrocer's' - 'the produce shop'

TT I -13 -'dawdle' - to linger

-'limpid' - 'clear as crystal'

TT I -13 -'pernickety' - 'wanting everything just right'

TT I - 14 -'unremarkable' - 'ordinary- looking'

-'retorted' - 'replied'

-'wump' - 'a worthless lump'

-'punctual' - 'on time'

TT I - 15 -'gloat'- 'look at with nasty satisfaction'

-'chaise longue' - an old-fashioned sofa

TT I - 17 -'skulking off' 'sneaking away'

TT I - 19 -'slumped' 'fell back heavily'

TT I - 21 -'belching' - noisily pushing up clouds of smoke

Telephone Tales II glossary on following page...

Telephone Tales II

TT II - 2 -'eaves' the underside of the jutting-out part of a

roof

TT II - 3 -'lantern-jawed' - having long thin jaws and chin

-'at the prospect of seeing' - 'at the thought they

would be seeing'

TT II - 4 -'cavorted to' - 'pranced about in time to (the

music)'

-'telemarketing' - selling by telephone

TT II - 5 -'aquatic' - 'living in water'

TT II - 9 -'milled edge' - 'having regular markings all

round the edge

TT II - 10 -'minting' - making coins

TT II - 11 -'dapper' - neat and sprightly

TT II - 13 -'sallied out' - went out of the house

TT II - 14 -'prediction' - 'telling the future'

-'accosting' - 'approaching and boldly talking to'

-'commended him' - 'praised him'

TT II - 15 -'broth' - a thin, tasty soup of meat or fish

TT II - 19 -'gourd' - the hollow, dried skin of the gourd

fruit

-'sleek' - looking well-fed and comfortable

TT II - 20 -'prone to' - 'likely to get'

TT II - 21 -'inflating' - 'swelling'

TT II - 22 -'menace' -'danger'

-'skirmish' - an unplanned bit of fighting

between small groups belonging to larger army

or naval forces

TT II - 24 -'Ferrari'- a very, very posh Italian sports car

TT II - 25 -'pandered to' - 'gave way to'

Here is space for more new words and their meanings >

......

....

....

Contents

Telephone Tales - I

List of Telephone Tales - II

Telephone Tales I – No 1

Holey MacRoary

Holey MacRoary was a big, ugly, hairy troll. You know, a sort of hobgoblin. Not many people had seen him, as he came out mainly at night and he didn't use his deep, booming voice very often. The folk in the pretty countryside were anyway not too keen to catch sight of him if they could help it, since he was rumoured to be able to cast spells and turn people into animals. After all, who would want to become a donkey (*sound*), or a long-horned

1

sheep (*sound*), or perhaps a savage little shrew *(sssssss - t ps pst)?*

But they knew where he lived, and that was in a dark cave that had once served as an ice-house; before they had refrigerators. It was way out in the country, in a gloomy hollow next to a wood. A pack-horse trail led past it, but now that they had roads in those parts, pack-horses weren't used any more than ice-houses were. So the big troll didn't get many visits. Some of the few passers-by had however thought they'd heard a distant rumbling sound, like a big animal snoring deep below *(sound)*.

Question: Why was he called Holey MacRoary? Before I tell you, you should know that some brave children had once seen him coming out of his cave in a shabby old raincoat. Now he was good and kind and never hurt anyone. So was his name Holey because he was good enough to be a saintly sort of troll? Most people weren't anxious to find out for sure, in case he turned out to be more nasty than saintly and cast an unwelcome spell on them.

A pity, because Holey MacRoary really liked company and would have been very nice to people if only they had dropped by. He even had business cards ready to give visitors. They had no address on them, just his name and title — 'Holey MacRoary. Troll'.

And what about the 'Mac' in his name? Had his folks come from Scotland? Or did the Roary part mean he was really an Irish kind of troll, like a leprechaun?

You've been very patient and deserve to have the answers.

If anyone had ever dropped by Holey MacRoary's cave and asked about his name, he would politely have explained that he was called 'Holey' not because he was saintly but because he lived in a hole. 'Mac' was in his name not because his Dad had come from Scotland but because, as the children had seen, he wore an old

macintosh. And the 'Roary' part of his name wasn't Irish.

He was called 'Roary' because, as I've already hinted, he

roared as he snored, as he roared as he snored *(slowly*

diminishing sound) …snored…roared…snored.

So now you know.

……………

Telephone Tales I – No 2

The Non-Tipping Chair

"Aha!" said Aunt Crotchety triumphantly — "I knew you'd fall off that chair if you climbed on to it without my helping you." Little Mim looked up at her from the floor. She hadn't really hurt herself as it had tipped over, but she had bumped her backside a bit. She felt more hurt at not having got at what she'd been after, namely the ice-cream in the freezer, before she tipped over.

"Aunt Crotchety" Mim declared "I didn't break anything, not even the chair. One day, I'm going to make a chair that doesn't flip over backwards, even if you push it. I'll make lots of those chairs and people will buy them and I'll become very rich and then I can have all the ice-cream I want. I'll keep it in an enormous ice-box on the floor so I won't have to climb on anything to get it — not even on one of my own tip-proof chairs that doesn't flip over backwards.

When Mim had last been to the Zoo, one of the animals had reminded her of someone she knew, but she couldn't think which or who. Aunt Crotchety was very tall; much taller than Mim's Mom. She had a long, long neck and a big nose that jutted out, and the rest of her was long and thin too. Today she was wearing a long yellow dress. She sniffed impatiently *(sound)* and pulled Mim off the floor, and plonked her back in her chair. "Now you stay

6

there until your Mom comes home. I'll check the ice-cream

in the freezer but you're not to have any till dinner-time."

Aunt Crotchety reached up to check the chocolate

ice-cream in the back of the tall freezer. Unfortunately,

when she reached into it, some of the other packages inside

tumbled out, as well as the ice-cream bucket *(sound of*

packages falling). Some of the chocolate ice-cream fell out

- splat - and made large brown spots all over Aunt

Crotchety's yellow dress. Mim couldn't help laughing and

clapping her hands. Now she knew exactly who the

mother-giraffe at the Zoo reminded her of.

. . . .

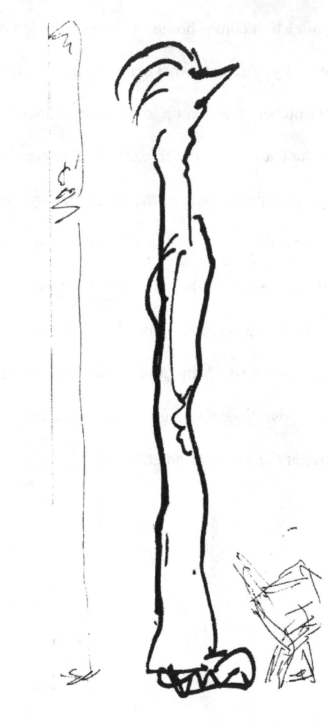

Big Snorter

No-one in the village had seen a dragon before. So
when Jim the mailman got to 123 Daisy Lane on his
morning round, he was surprised to see this one asleep on
the lawn. It was much bigger and shinier than an alligator,
more like a dinosaur. It had huge scaly wings folded back,
a long green tail and tall ears cocked like a mule's. Steam
came slowly from its nose. A low rumbling in its throat
every now and again got louder and turned into a sneezy,

deafening cough *(sound)*. That's why some people called him "Big Snorter".

Jim had only one letter for 123 Daisy Lane. Glancing down, he saw that it was in fact addressed to 'Mr Big Snorter.' So, very gently, he nudged the dragon behind the ear- got ready to jump in case of trouble and handed over the envelope. Big Snorter woke up slowly, yawned *(sound),* and in a dee-eep voice muttered "Sorry, I'm a bit tired from yesterday. A nasty mule kicked me in the shin so I had to eat 'im. He tasted better than I expected but I got indigestion and slept badly". He opened his letter. "Oh dear! More junk mail!...Why should I of all people want to buy a motorbike? I can fly anywhere I want much quicker. Watch!"

"Upon which he unfolded his scaly wings and, snorting loudly *(sound),* flew gracefully twice round the oak tree in the middle of the lawn. Then he settled down in front of Jim and asked, hesitatingly," I get so little

interesting mail. D'you think you could bring me a nice

letter from someone next time, instead of this awful junk

stuff? And could you please make it soon, as I have to be

moving on?"

Jim was doubtful, but didn't want to disappoint such

a polite dragon. So he said "Big Snorter, I can't usually

choose what mail I bring. But since it's you, and you took

the trouble to show me how gracefully you fly, I'll write

you a nice letter myself and bring it next Monday. Bye,

Bye Big Snorter"

Then, with the sound of sneezing/snorting fading in

the distance *(sound),* he walked on to the next house he had

letters for.

. . . .

Telephone Tales I – No 4

Dog Molecule

"Just because I'm small doesn't mean I can't be fierce" confided dog Molecule to his friend next door, poodle-dog Gwendoline. "After all, how did I handle that ugly hunk of a guy who said he'd come to repair the telephone?"

"Though no-one could tell at the time, I did have a bit of a problem with that man. It wasn't his size that worried me. The thing is that, as you know, I lurve to chew on that leather bone Mom gave me for my birthday. She'd hidden it before she went out. It was now my chewing time and this man's shoes smelled just like my leather bone! Here was I, trusty dog Molecule, responsible for the safety of everyone who lived at our home. Of course I'm not allowed to bite visitors unless they misbehave. Yet here was this man who had so far behaved himself but whose shoes were just asking to be chewed. What would you have done, friend Gwendoline?"

"Well, I had a stroke of luck. The repairman had to put on his work boots to climb the telephone pole along the street. He left his shoes in the hall and, the moment he was out the door, I grabbed one of them and hid it in the closet. I would have taken them both but they were so enormous, one was all I could manage in one grab. It tasted so super that I had to growl fiercely as I chewed it *(sound)*. I had counted on just a brief chew, to keep me going until I had my own leather bone. But before I could put the shoe back,

the man opened the door. What a problem for me,

Gwendoline!

Again, luck was with me. The man glanced down at

the one shoe lying where he'd left it, and then at me. I was

expecting beeg trouble and could only growl in a worried

sort of way *(sound)*. But Mom was now back and all he

said to her was "Hey, Mam, those working shoes of mine

are getting so worn that it's time the firm bought me a new

pair. Could I bother you to toss this one, and the other shoe

when it turns up, into your trash can?"

I thought I saw a twinkle in his eye as he left, saying,

"So long, Molecule. Have a good growl!"

. . . .

Telephone Tales I – No 5

Told by William the Worm

"'What a measly little worm that Gregory is!' I heard Aunt Crotchety exclaim when she had caught her neighbor's child Gregory trying to kick Moggins, her cat. Now, being a worm myself, I wasn't too pleased to hear that sort of talk. And though I'm not above ground very often so as to be able to hear people talking, that wasn't the first time I've heard nasty things being said about worms."

"So just let me tell you about some of the good things we worms do. First of all, we provide the best possible food for all the lovely birds you have in your garden. Mind you, I'd rather it be one of my friends rather than I who provides the bird food. But think how much cooler it is to be able to offer breakfast to, say, a pretty sap-sucker or a Jenny Wren than to be run over crossing the road, as so many unfortunate kids are nowadays when they don't look both ways first. And then I was quite proud one day to overhear our worthy police chief, Captain Trumpet, - who loves in his spare time to go fishing - proclaim how much better worms are as bait than anything else."

"But let me tell you about the most important thing of all we do for you. Maybe you'll never know if I don't share it with you. What we do so well is to improve the soil in which things grow; yes just about anything, - trees, bushes, grass, pineapples, grapes, daisies, whortleberries,

17

strawberries, boysenberries - they all grow better when we

worms have had a chance to work at the soil underground.

And that includes your favorite ice-cream too; since the best

ice-cream is made from the milk of cows, who produce it

only by eating grass. And you can tell Aunt Crotchety,

should you ever be unlucky enough to meet her, that the

same applies to her favorite beer and beef-steak, both of

which like milk depend very much on what grows in the

soil!"

"So if you should ever be out in your yard, or

somebody else's, and you spot a lively worm wriggling

away on the ground, remember how useful he is and be

careful not to tread on him. It might be me, William!"

. . . .

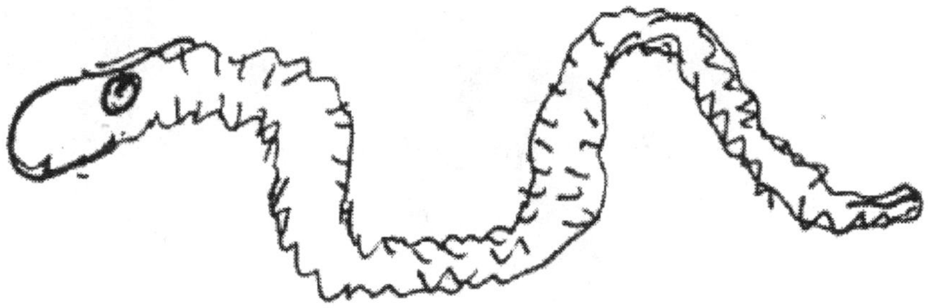

Telephone Tales I – No 6

Willy Jim and Woops

Willy Jim lives in the country. Last month, he got a BB gun for his birthday. How he loved that gun! He banged away for hours at targets in his folks' back yard. But when his Dad discovered Willy Jim was using precious file boxes as targets, he told him to get into the adjoining field and practise there.

So Willy Jim took his BB gun into the field. Perhaps he'd be lucky and find a rabbit taking a snooze, or a fat

20

crow guzzling corn, waiting for him to take pot shots at them. But there were no crows, no rabbits; no quail; no foxes; no prairie dogs; no watermelons; nothing worth shooting at. So he went on to the next field, which had a fine white fence round it.

This time he reckoned he'd struck lucky. Some of Farmer Growler's best dairy cows were grazing beyond the fence. Willy Jim picked out one cow whose name was Woops, but of course he didn't know that then. She was a bit far off but he chose her because she was mostly black with a big white patch on her side. "What a great target" he thought, and aimed at the middle of her white patch. "Bang!" Because of the distance, his BB carried only far enough to tap Woops gently on her side, but in the dead center of her white patch. She felt the 'ping' only enough to dance a clumsy step or two away.

Willie Jim felt pretty pleased with his master shot and was just going home to tell his folks when, suddenly, a voice of thunder bellowed "What do you think you're doing to my prize Holsteins, you little so and so?" It was Farmer Growler himself, and he wasn't pleased. You can imagine that when Farmer Growler visited and complained, Wille Jim's Dad wasn't happy either. So, for shooting Woops and probably making her milk turn sour, Willie Jim had to do without his BB gun for all of two weeks, and without his bicycle too.

Since then, he's made sure never to shoot at Woops or her sisters but always safely and at a proper target. In fact, he knew he'd acted stupidly and by way of saying 'Sorry', he bought some lovely marshmallows with his own pocket money and gave them to Farmer Growler to pass on to Woops. Farmer Growler was quite surprised and reckoned Willie Jim wasn't so bad after all. Between you and me, after tasting the marshmallows to make sure they weren't harmful to animals, he found there weren't any left for Woops herself.

....

Beastlet

There once was a guinea-pig who liked to eat, -

almost non-stop; hay, grass pellets, carrots, lettuce, kiwi

fruit; and some things we'd throw away, like melon rind

and banana peel. He wouldn't touch grapes but he loved

their stalks. So you'd probably not like his lunch much.

He'd turn away in disgust at any sort of meat.

A nice thing about guinea-pigs is they're not very

noisy. If they're hungry, they squeak a little, to say 'Please bring me some of the food I like; and please hurry '(*sound*).

Should they become scared,- perhaps of getting hurt,- they

give a much louder, piercing squeal you can't miss hearing

(sound).

But if a guinea-pig feels really happy, like if he's

being stroked on his back or under his chin, he chuckles

deep inside *(sound)*. Anyway, the guinea-pig we had,

whose name was 'Beastlet', ate and chuckled a lot. His

jowls and coat and whiskers glowed and he became fat and

comfortable, like a small City Councilman.

When we went swimming in our pool, we often put

him in a little open tub, with a carrot, and sent him sailing.

He was nervous at first at the rocking motion, but he soon

learned to keep still and enjoy the view.

When the weather got really warm, we lowered him

gently into the water and made him swim from one of us to

the other.

His nub-like legs would paddle furiously and he swam quite fast until his fur coat got waterlogged and he began to sink. We never let his nose go under the water. We'd always place a helping hand in time under his fat little belly; lift him out, towel him off and dry him in the sun in a tubful of fresh hay. He'd go to sleep with his eyes open and when he woke, we'd treat him to a dried leaf for being so brave.

This may be a pretty boring story, but guinea pigs that are house pets don't lead very exciting lives, and that's how they like it. A quick swim in the pool is as big a thrill as comes their way, except when they get to chew a grape stem or someone really nice like you comes to pet them. Yet, who knows? Quiet though they look, perhaps they're thinking really exciting thoughts underneath. What's your guess?

Better luck next time, when I might have a dragon story for you.

....

Telephone Tales I – No 8

The Mechanical Ostrich

(Told by Geordie)

When Suzy my sister and I asked our Dad what Santa might bring us for Christmas, he wasn't sure. Suzy had spilled blueberry jelly over his white jacket, and I hadn't tidied my room or fed dog Molecule, even though I'd promised. So Dad said the best he could do was ask Santa to bring us a mechanical ostrich. We really hadn't been good enough to deserve anything else. It would be a test. If we looked after it carefully every day, then maybe Santa

might do better for us next year.

When I'd gone to bed, I heard a whirring noise

(sound). The bedroom door opened and, believe it or not, in

strutted a great big mechanical ostrich. It looked rather like

Aunt Crotchety but was even taller. With every step, it

plonked its huge feet one in front of the other with a big

'clank' *(sound)*. Now and again it lifted and shook its big

feathers (like Aunt Crotchety dusting the piano - *(sound)*.

Its big eyes like black and yellow billiard balls looked

straight at me. Imagine how scary that was! And then it

talked, in a rusty, croaky voice "Geordie (that's me), are

you going to bring me my coffee and comb my feathers,

and stroke my neck in the mornings? And wind me up

twenty times like it says in the instructions so I can keep

going, - because I don't use batteries? And bring me a box

of sand to hide my head in, like a proper ostrich?

(In case you had'nt heard, ostriches are supposed to hide their heads in sand if trouble comes). I knew Dad wouldn't like it if I promised the mechanical ostrich things and didn't do them. So I answered, "Dear mechanical ostrich, please remember I'm only a little guy and I'll need a helping hand. Aunt Crotchety's the only one of us tall enough to stroke your neck in the mornings. But if you help Suzy and me push the lawnmower, and pitch in with me tidying my room, and go with me walking dog Molecule, I'll do my darnedest to wind you up and look after you".

Just then, Mom burst into the room. "Geordie, wake up! Hurry or you'll be late for school!".

Well, I can't explain it, but from that moment on, I had much less problem doing my chores. I could feel Mechanical Ostrich, no longer scary anymore, looking down at me like a big uncle with black and yellow billiard-ball eyes, and making everything so much easier for me.

Christmas came and Santa brought Suzy and me super bicycles. So you'll understand why, ever since, I've not only missed my feathery friend but I've always seen Santa's sleigh as drawn not by a bunch of old reindeer but by one, huge, foot-clanking, cool, long-striding mechanical ostrich with billiard-ball eyes.

Telephone Tales I – No 9

I Hear Voices

"Why do some people sound so nice when they speak, while others sound awful?" Geordie asked his sister Suzy. "I always like to hear Jim the mailman say "Hi, there!" He's got such a cool and gentle voice. Not like Captain Trumpet, our police chief. He talks like our lawnmower going flat out *(sound)*. And Gran'pa Thrush round the corner reminds me of our backyard shed door opening when he says anything *(rusty sound)* - perhaps

33

because he's so old. Voices do change when they get real

old. On the 'phone last week, Dad mistook great-Uncle

Hank for Aunt Daisy and told him how much he liked him

in her new pink dress.

"Yes," Suzy agreed, "I get those two mixed up on the

phone, too. But I like nice voices. Yet isn't it funny that

people with yucky voices can sometimes sound great when

they sing? Aunt Crotchety sounds like a grackel when she

talks (*sound*). But remember last Sunday in church! I

thought it was Miss Stringit, our music teacher at school,

singing the hymn so beautifully behind us (*sound*). But I

looked round and it was Aunt Crotchety! She didn't seem

to figure out why I looked so surprised."

"Maybe God gave Aunt Crotchety a pretty singing

voice because He wasn't too kind to her in other ways."

Geordie went on. "Now Captain Trumpet probably got his

loud and growly voice because he's police chief and can do

fun things others mustn't - like breaking the speed limit. It wouldn't be fair if some folks had everything! Same with you, a bit, too, Suzy, if I may say so! Sometimes you're pretty mean to me like when you hide the sugar at breakfast; but you do sound nice when you speak - when you don't talk too loud. I don't think Miss Stringit's done much so far to help you with your singing, though. Why not ask Aunt Crotchety to run through 'Day of wrath and doom impending' with you before church next Sunday? That's her favorite hymn. I'll bet she'll be surprised!"

. . . .

Telephone Tales I – No 10

With a wild Pig, watch out!

We had a wild pig at home once. No, not my classmate Gregory who kicked Aunt Crotchety's cat at my birthday party; but a real wild pig, with four legs. When we were living in South America, Dad brought it home from the jungle. After straying from its herd, it had been cared for by a local lady at her farm. So it had already lived with humans and wasn't exactly savage. But with wild animals, you never know. And this one, a full-grown peccary, had long front teeth as sharp as Dad's razor.

doña Pancha, as Dad named her, seemed really to take to us. We had fun bathing her in our little plastic pool. She loved and usually managed to swallow the big bar of soap we used. We took her for walks to the village in her leather harness. The locals crossed to the other side of the road. They had a healthy respect for wild beasts and weren't sure if doña Pancha would be as friendly to them as she was to us.

At first, when Dad let her out of her pen into the garden, he had his shotgun ready, in case she misbehaved. But she never hurt us. She could run faster and jump further than any of us, even dog Hamish our Labrador, and she loved to play. Only Francisco the gardener didn't return her affection because she always ate his carnations.

He would push his pitchfork at her and shout "Váya-te!"

("Go away!") *(imitate)*.

One evening, we went to see why doña Pancha wasn't coming out to play. We found her lying on her side in the old stable where she lived, barely breathing, her eyes all but glazed over. The veterinarian when he arrived said she was critically ill with pneumonia. In the jungle areas where she came from, even in winter it never got as cold as where we now lived, high in the mountains. Every evening he gave her powerful penicillin shots. But she just lay there, sick and still; and we worried.

At the vet's fifth visit, he was about to plunge his enormous syringe into her backside as usual when, - like lightning her head twisted back. He whipped his hand away only just in time to avoid losing a finger from the vicious snap of her jaws *(sound)*. He said "I see I'm not needed here any more," put all his things back into his Gladstone bag, and left. Happily, we didn't need him any more all the time we were in South America.

And what happened to her when we left? Well, that's another story!

doña Pancha and the Sick Boys

I told you about doña Pancha our pet javelina,
remember? Well, this is what happened when my younger
brother and I were in bed with colds. We lived in a big
Spanish house which had parquet floors; the kind with
interlacing wooden blocks, - stylish but slippery if you
don't watch out. doña Pancha was not allowed inside,
partly because Mom and Dad didn't want any outside
animals there, and because doña Pancha's hooves couldn't

easily manage those floors without skidding. (A bit like us walking on ice!)

We weren't very sick and had got bored looking at books. So when we heard a scuffling outside our upstairs bedroom door *(sound),* we wondered what on earth it could be. Imagine our surprise when the door pushed open and there was doña Pancha! She walked unsteadily into the room and lay down on the runner rug between our beds - with her front legs flat in front and her hind legs flat behind and her chin flat on the floor; showing she felt really secure and comfortable. We were a bit worried she'd get into trouble with Dad for being there, but couldn't help being glad she'd made the effort to come to us. We reached down and patted her on the head and she grunted happily *(sound).*

It turned out that doña Pancha by pushing with her powerful snout had forced open the little gate to the old stable she lived in.

And then she'd crept through the open kitchen door while no-one was looking and had somehow got up the stairs. How she found us, I don't know. Maybe she knew our scent so well by then that she just followed her long nose.

Mom and Dad had been looking for doña Pancha all over the property and weren't too pleased when they discovered where she was. They thought at first that we'd brought her up. Dad quickly put her under his arm and carried her downstairs. He had to talk sternly to her about again disobeying orders but Mom and he were quite touched she had gone to all that trouble to visit us when we were sick. So she got off lightly that time.

And we realised we had a true friend in doña Pancha!

. . . .

Telephone Tales I – No 12

Doris and the Green Lizards

When Geordie was just a little guy, one of the things he most wanted, even more than ice cream, was a pet green lizard. So he was delighted when, one Christmas, Santa brought him three, foot-long lovely green lizards. He called them Shem, Ham and Japhet. He kept them in a shallow glass tank and fed them lettuce and insects and scraps. They seemed happy enough but probably missed the luxurious green foliage of their native habitat a little.

Geordie couldn't do much about that except that, one day, he was told to fetch some bushy green herbs from the greengrocers for the dinner his Mom and Dad were giving for some important guests.

A young lady called Doris was to serve at dinner. It was her first time and she listened carefully to all the things she had to do; whom to serve first; how to pass the dishes; change the plates; fill the glasses and so on. You know there are lots of things like that to remember when you're entertaining guests.

Doris felt at ease in her smart maid's uniform, with its pretty sleeves puffed at the elbow, and she began to think that serving at table was no big deal. She went over all the things for the main course and started proudly carrying in the best family porcelain plates, piled high on a big silver tray. Suddenly, from nowhere, three cold clammy shapes flopped on to her bare forearm.

She gave a terrible shreik, dropped everything and fled into the kitchen ready to die. Geordie, upstairs in bed, heard the terrible shreik and crash of crockery and came running down. He soon figured out that Shem, Ham and Japhet had got out of their tank into the bushy green herbs he'd placed next to it, and from there, seeking adventure, they'd climbed up the dining room door. They didn't like the top of the door once they'd got there and decided that Doris's forearm passing below was much more inviting.

You can believe that those lizards ruined the dinner as well as the family porcelain. So Geordie and they weren't exactly popular. The lizards had to be put in the shed. But they didn't mind because the shed was next to the garden and they saw lots of nice chances of escaping into more bushy herbs.

. . . .

Telephone Tales I – No 13

Miss Trundle and the Traffic Cop

Unless she was late getting up, Suzy usually walked to school. It wasn't far and the traffic was generally light. There were only two traffic signals on the way and she was always sensible enough to wait until there was someone else to cross with.

This particular morning, she hadn't dawdled over breakfast; the birds were singing (*Sound*); the morning sky was limpid blue; nasty classmate Gregory was late so she didn't have to walk with him; everything was fine. She had even done her homework - without too much help from her Dad - and was carrying it to school with her. For once, she was actually looking forward to handing it in to her teacher, the pernickety Miss Scratchit.

The lights were down that morning at the second big intersection and the traffic was being directed by a police officer she hadn't seen before. He was fat and pompous. He got impatient with one driver who hadn't understood his signals and kept the traffic waiting while he yelled at him. (*Sound of traffic noise and of policeman's yelling at the driver -*).

At that moment, Suzy was joined by old Miss Trundle, who lived in the same subdivision. Old Miss trundle was a tiny lady, a bit sharp with people sometimes, but really quite sweet in her way. "Hello, Miss Trundle" said Suzy. "Thanks again for buying that box of Girl Scout cookies". She took Suzy's arm and they were both some way across the roadway when the fat policemen held up his hand. Rather than turn back to the sidewwalk and risk being held up heavens knew how much longer, they decided to walk on as far as the median. The traffic cop still held up his hand.

As they approached, the cop sternly addressed Miss Trundle. "Lady, don't you know what it means when I hold up my hand?" "I ought to" snapped Miss Trundle "I taught school for thirty years. Yes, you may go to the restroom if you like".

....

The Witch and the Clockabill (Part One)

Once there was an unremarkable dragon called
Rumbold. He lived near a witch called Sniff. Sniff was a
busybody. Rumbold was like most dragons - bone lazy. He
liked to loll about in his deep dark cave. At noon, he would
yawn and emit sleepy streams of smoke from his nostrils
and scratch behind his ear with a hind foot; pick his many
long teeth with one great claw; and begin to think about
breakfast. By that time Sniff, having already put in half a

day's busybodying, was feeling tired and even readier than usual to criticize.

One day as she bustled past the entrance to the cave, she yelled in," Rumbold, if you don't start getting up at the proper time and do something useful, I'll turn you into a dragon". Rumbold retorted "I already am a dragon". So Sniff said "Then I'll turn you into a toad" Rumbold replied" I'd love being a toad ‒ all I'd have to do is hop around catching flies, which is a lot easier than being a dragon. If a dragon wants a decent meal, he has to fly out and capture a fat ox or a slender maiden; and that's a lot of trouble and makes him unpopular and he has to watch out for knights in shining armor coming to do him in. I'd lurve to be a nice, peaceful toad."

"Oh very well, you wump" said Sniff. "But at least you've got to become punctual. I'm turning you into a clockabill" So with a wave of her magic wand, she zapped

him and went home for her nap.

At first Rumbold didn't feel different and he thought

mouldy old Sniff had lost her touch. Then, glancing into

his cave mirror, he saw his eyes had become huge alarm

clocks. He opened his big toothy mouth to roar in surprise,

but instead of a roar, all that came out of his throat was the

sound of a clock ticking (sound). So he snapped his jaws

shut *(sound)*. But he didn't want to miss his nap, and slept

a whole hour. Then, suddenly, the alarm went off in his

head *(sound)* and of course he woke up. He settled down to

sleep again but of course the same thing happened (sound).

And so on, and on.

For what happens next, you've got to wait till the

next story.

. . . .

The Witch and the Clockabill (Part Two)

Now lazy Rumbold-turned-clockabill might be, but he wasn't dumb. He decided to make the best of things and since he now had masses of spare time awake, he learned to play cards. When he got too good at solitaire, he took up crossword puzzles. When he'd done even the hardest and knew all the words in the dictionary, he studied finance like his rich uncle Arbuthnot had, and soon got rich too.

Sniff the witch, being a mean old thing, and knowing that Rumbold-turned-clockabill wasn't now sleeping as often as he had liked to do before, decided to visit him and gloat. But imagine her surprise when she saw his cave now! Being rich, he'd paid to have it made into the most beautiful of all the caves in the world, with music, gardens, flowers, giant-screen TV, air-conditioning, pretty birds, and fountains endlessly spouting root beer.

Sniff found him lolling comfortably in his chaise-longue by the swimming-pool which was filled with hip, laughing maidens. They were quite safe because he'd become a vegetarian since he'd studied and got rich. For lunch, he now preferred mangos to maidens. He was talking to his stockbroker on his cellular phone. With the other claw he punched numbers into a smart notebook computer balanced on his scaly green belly. Behind the bushes, she could see a sleek red open sports car. "Howdy, Sniffie? "he said.

Sniff looked enviously at all the lovely flowers and the shimmering pool and the endless fountains of root beer and the sleek red open sports car and thought "Instead of turning him into a toad or back into a dragon, maybe I'll turn myself into one of those hip, slender laughing maidens." And so she did.

Geordie the Gargoyle

Geordie was making faces at Suzy in the back of the

car. Usually he was a good older brother. He'd taught her

to tie her shoes only the week before. But now, Suzy

started crying. "Whatever you're doing," said Dad, who

was driving, "Stop it!". Suzy sniffed and wiped away a

tear. Geordie was good for about ten minutes. Then he put

his face right in front of Suzy's, crossed his eyes, opened

his mouth so that all his teeth showed, and stuck out his

tongue as far as it would go. Suzy started wailing again *(sound)*.

Dad glanced in the rear view mirror in time to see the awful face that had started Suzy crying again. 'D'you remember our trip to Farnham Abbey in England?" he asked. "Nope" said Geordie. "Yes, you do - it was that old, old church where stone monsters were sitting all round the edge of the roof with their mouths open. As we went in to church, it was sunny. When we came out, it was raining hard and water from the roof was pouring from the monsters' mouths". "Now I remember" said Geordy. "I thought they were neat and wanted to watch them longer, but you didn't want us out in the rain. What were they called, now?"

"They were Gargoyles" said Dad "D'you know how they got to be on the roof?" "Not a clue? Long ago, some boys your age were seeing which of them could make the

58

ugliest face to scare their little sisters the most. Just as they were puffing their cheeks and wiggling their ears and squinting and stretching their tongues the farthest, it started raining. Suddenly, a terrible flash of lightning rent the sky, and all the boys vanished."

"It was a while before people looked up and saw the boys, all turned into stone, perched on the edge of the roof, making faces not only at their little sisters but at all who passed below. They were left up on the church roof because that was where most people would recognize them for the silly nitwits they were to want to frighten their small sisters. But should the same thing, Heaven forbid, ever happen to you, we'll stick you on the dining-room mantelpiece, and you'll be able to watch us eating hamburgers and ice-cream; - while poor you can have nothing because you're a gargoyle."

"Well", said Geordie, rather impressed, and finally letting his cheeks in. "Maybe it'd be cool being a gargoyle… but only till lunchtime".

……………

The Chorus Fable

You know what a fable is? It's a made-up story, usually about animals doing wrong or stupid things just like humans. It's meant to show us humans how dumb we are to behave like that, and perhaps save us the embarassment of having to learn from our own mistakes. You may have been told the old fable about the fox looking up longingly at some lovely ripe grapes hanging on their vine; then jumping up at them desperately but finding them too high for him to reach; and then skulking off with the excuse that they weren't worth getting anyway because they were too sour! The moral of that story is that the fox was certainly no sport!

Well here is a new fable. Once upon a time, a big grackle flew by mistake into a church, and was so taken with the gorgeous sound of the choir that he decided to sing along with them. He opened his big grey beak and sang, too, at the top of his voice. (*sound*) The choirmaster stopped the choir and said "Somebody's making a terrible noise. Will they please shut up?"

So the grackle went back to his friends in their favorite oak tree, and they all sang together as loud as they could. They thought they were making lovely music. Passers-by would of course have preferred to hear a mocking-bird, but at least nobody told them to shut up.

The moral of this story is, if you have a long black tail and a long grey beak and sound like a grackle, you don't need to go to church. If you feel you'd like to do so all the same, you'll be welcome; but make sure you keep quiet unless the choir director has a long grey beak and a long black tail and sounds like you do.

. . . .

Telephone Tales I – No 18

The Grackle and the Mockingbird

Once upon a time there was a mockingbird that loved to sing in the moonlight. *(sound)* His song was so beautiful that everyone would stay up late just to hear. One of the mockingbird's admirers was a big, black grackle. She thought to herself "The mockingbird sits on the highest TV antenna, a great location - and that's why everybody listens".

So the next night, the grackle got to the antenna before the Mocker and began to sing her grackle song. (*sound*) Soon there were hoots and howls from all the residents within earshot, and they tossed old boots and rotten fruit at the grackle to make her stop. Somebody yelled "That grackle sounds like a rusty machine!". The grackle was pleased, for she liked audience participation; and she thought the sound of rusty machinery much nicer than the song of the mockingbird; and she loved rotten fruit even more than that.

So she stopped singing and gladly flew down to feast on the fruit. The mockingbird had been sitting nearby watching the whole performance. "Well," she said, smiling, "You certainly got what you deserved!" — "Yes, thank you very much", happily replied the grackle, who had eaten her fill and was now tearing out laces from an old boot to add to her nest. "You can have the antenna now, I'm finished for the evening".

So does this story carry any moral for us, like the fables of the fox and the grapes, and the hare and the tortoise do? Frankly, I'm not sure. But first, it might tell us that a good location isn't always everything; second, that there's no accounting for tastes; and thirdly, that even when things don't look too good, the problem may have a bright side for somebody. On the other hand, if too many old boots and rotten fruit give us indigestion, then it's maybe time to change our tune.

. . . .

Telephone Tales I – No 19

Why Geordie was late for School

Geordie wasn't exactly a model student. Sometimes, when practising how to frighten his little sister, he twisted his face into such awful shapes that his teacher Miss Scratchit was afraid it might never return to normal. But he usually paid enough attention in class to be able to coach his Dad how to help him with his homework afterwards. And he was up early enough most mornings to catch the school bus.

But not every morning. One day, he missed the bus and was racing along so as not to be late when, far off, he saw a big lout from the other school push somebody over and run away with something. When he ran up, he saw poor old Gertrude sitting on the sidewalk. Gertrude was elderly and handicapped and couldn't talk too well. She really was poor and old and Geordie couldn't understand why anyone would want to push her over. Surely she didn't have anything worth stealing. He tried to help her up but she was too heavy and slumped back on to the sidewalk again. So he gave her his lunch and was running as fast as he could towards school when he saw police Chief Trumpet across the road. He had to shout several times about Gertrude before the Captain heard; and what with that and everything else, he was quite late for class.

Miss Scratchit didn't believe him at first because she knew old Gertrude was supposed to stay at home; and she thought he was making up his story. But then Captain Trumpet telephoned to say that Gertrude had been fetching a package from the post office, and Geordie had not only tried to help her up, but had given her his lunch as well. So Geordie was excused for being late and treated to a special cafeteria lunch - which actually tasted better than his Mom's usually did. In fact he felt quite good about his morning, espccially as he heard they'd nailed the thug who'd pushed poor Gertrude over.

Maybe something like this will happen again, he thought, but can the cafeteria be trusted to give me as great a lunch as this another time?

. . . .

The Blue Racer

Geordie and his kid sister Suzy were really fond of Josh, the foreman at Uncle Pickle's ranch where they sometimes spent the week-end. Josh used to show them all sorts of fun country things they'd never get to see back home. As well as cows and horses, he liked wild animals and wanted his friends to understand them too. One day, Josh took them in the jeep to look at a straggly 'possum nest in the far wood.

"If I'd built that nest" cried Suzy, I'd have been more careful to make it clean and neat". "Well," said Josh" maybe you build the possum a real neat one next to his, and see if he prefers yours".

They had to drive on and see how high the creek was. It hadn't rained and the cows in that part of the ranch needed it to drink from. On the way, they spotted a vulture flying high above, and a fox trotting in the distance. "Let's hope they haven't been after our new chicks!" said Josh.

As they were getting out of the Jeep near the barn Geordie and Suzy had a terrible shock. A shiny long dark-blue shape whipped out from behind the car, raced almost over their feet and disappeared under the barn door. Suzy screamed and Geordie looked for a stick; but Josh told them, "It's OK, guys. That was a 'Blue Racer'. It's one of the nicest snakes around. It's a pretty color and it's not a bit poisonous; in fact, it eats the rats and other vermin which

71

give us so much trouble on the ranch; it kills the venomous snakes we do need to watch out for; and, believe it or not, like a dog it'll sometimes follow us humans a while as we walk along, as if for company."

Suzy felt better after hearing that and thought it was a pity there weren't any Blue Racers at home. Otherwise she'd certainly have taken one to school and invited her teacher, Miss Scratchit, to take it for a walk.

....

Geordie the Chef.

Geordie was home by himself. Aunt Crotchety was away, Mom was away, and his Dad had called to say he'd be home late. "Can you find something to eat? he'd asked. "Sure" said Geordie, "There's tons of food in the kitchen." "Leave the kitchen clean, now." warned his Dad. "Mother won't want to find it a mess." "Don't worry," said Geordie. His idea of dinner was cookies and ice-cream. But there was only one cookie left, and no ice cream. Bacon there

was in plenty in the fridge. And bacon he loved.

Geordie had never cooked before, but he'd often

watched Mom. He got out the largest frying-pan and put it

on the stove. He remembered seeing Mom use lard when

she fried things, so he turned the gas up high and put a huge

spoonful of the white stuff in the pan. He was still nervous

about burning the bacon so he put in two more spoonfuls.

The bacon package was family size. He peeled off

five long strips, laid them in the grease and enjoyed

watching them sizzling and spluttering and belching smoke

(sound). Once the bacon strips were small and brown and

curly, Geordie fished them out and let them drain on a paper

towel, as he'd seen Mom do. Then, though his eyes were

smarting in the smoke, he tasted:

"A bit cindery, perhaps, but eatable!" - In fact good

enough to fry another five slices.

74

When Mom came home, clouds of dark greasy smoke rolled out as she opened the door. Through the fume-filled kitchen, she could dimly see Geordie finishing the last of the half-pound of bacon. On the stove, the biggest frying-pan was brim-full of hot grease.

"Hi Mom", said Geordie. "I had bacon while you were out." "I can tell," said his Mom. In fact we're all going to be able to tell for days before the house stops reeking of bacon smoke! I'm only grateful you didn't set the whole house on fire! What a nice surprise for Dad to find it all burned down, and you inside all shrivelled up like the bacon! So much fat's bad for you, but if you've got to eat bacon, cook it on low heat. And it makes its own grease." "OK," said Geordie ruefully, "I'll remember. I thought I'd been smart to use that lard! I guess you've got to learn things the hard way"

But, secretly, he thought "What a pity, that cindery bacon didn't taste at all bad!".

. . . .

Bye Bye doña Pancha

I've already told you about doña Pancha, the pet wild pig we got to be so fond of in South America. I could tell you a lot more about her, but time's short so for now it'll just have to be how she coped with the sour plums in our garden, and what happened to her when we had to come home to America.

Our big garden was full of plum trees. They gave a lot of fruit but the plums were too sour to eat uncooked.

doña Pancha didn't mind them raw. She'd figured out a special way to eat them without wasting time. She went straight for them in the big heaps into which they'd fallen under each tree. Slurping up each plum noisily on one side of her big mouth, she crunched super-quick for a second then spat out the stone from the other side. But before she had quite done doing that, she was into another plum; and so it went on, suck, - chew - and spit-; like a high-speed robot. It really was something to see, - and hear *(sound)*.

Later on, Suzy and I had a go at the same technique with cooked plums at table. But Mom for some reason didn't like it much and made us stop, so we never got to practise enough to get up to doña Pancha's speed.

We couldn't take doña Pancha with us when the time arrived for us to go. A kind German lady, whose husband had a garden as big as a park, with a wood and lots of bushes and monkeys, agreed to let doña Pancha loose there.

But our pet was so sorry to be parted from us that she turned savage and with her razor-sharp teeth ripped up one of her new mistress's dogs. So doña Pancha had to be locked up in a great big dog pound they had, where she was miserable and howled with loneliness *(sound)*. We could hear her all the way from our house and it made us feel awful. But once we had gone, the lady found a nice family which had a male wild pig of the same sort as doña Pancha. And it wasn't very long before we heard that our dear old pet was expecting a family herself. I hope she taught her piglets how to eat sour plums.

. . . .

Telephone Tales I – No 23

Molly in the Dumps

Molly had the blues. Her best friend was moving.

She'd scored a 'C' on her last test. Her ankle was really

hurting from that kick she'd got at Soccer. She'd lost her

favorite blue handbag. She'd been told she'd have to go

slow on the ice cream if she wasn't to get fat and ugly.

Worse still, Sizzler Sockit, her favorite pop star, had been

taking drugs and got busted. How on earth to cheer up?

Mom, Dad and Uncle Pickle were all away. She didn't feel like opening up to just anyone. But, thinking it over, there was one person she thought she might visit. Greatgranny Periwinkle was so old she didn't have to be polite anymore; though spry she certainly was, and feisty. Only the other day, a hoodlum had tried to snatch her bag, but she'd poked him in the tummy so hard with her umbrella that he ran away gasping (*sound*). If she wanted ice cream at dinner, she had it. If she didn't like the Pastor's Sunday sermon, she told him. Some folk were a bit scared of Greatgran, but Molly thought she was fun, and they got on very well. She walked over and explained her problem.

Greatgran didn't waste time. "When I'm in the dumps", she said, "I go talk to someone who's much worse off than me.

Then I do that good turn I'd long been thinking of doing for a friend. Never mind if they don't thank you. It's the intention that counts. After that, I treat myself to the biggest popsicle around. Now get on with it. Here's a dollar to help. Bye!"

Molly chose poor old Gertrude, a handicapped lady, to call on, and told her about Sizzler Sockit. Gertrude said he deserved all he got, and seemed real glad Molly had bothered to stop by. After that, while thinking about a good turn to do, she saw some litter on Captain Trumpet's lawn. She was just picking it up for him when he yelled at her from his front door; "Stop littering my lawn!".

"Well, at least I tried" she thought as she went home and put a band-aid on Kitty Moggins's sore back leg. It wasn't much of a good deed but it was more than she'd been able to do for Captain Trumpet and, as Greatgran had said, it's the intention that counts! Then she remembered

83

there was a popsicle in the fridge. By the time she'd

finished it, Molly was a lot less sad, and she felt she'd done

the right thing visiting Greatgran.

The Old Farm (Part One)

Our neighbor Granpa Thrush once took Suzy and me,

Geordie, to his old house, way out in the sticks. His

grandad had grown up there, so you can imagine how old it

was. No-one lived in it now; it had been shut for years. We

were warned to take buckets and mops and brooms, and

flashlights because it didn't have electricity. We were

excited to see what sort of place it was, and, frankly, a bit

nervous about what we'd find.

Dad couldn't come but he gave me his stout walking stick in case of snakes. I'd used it once to kill a cottonmouth at Uncle Pickle's ranch. Mom had us bring hats in case bats got into our hair, and fly-swatters against spiders.

It took Granpa a while to find the right heavy key out of the big bunch he carried. Finally, the door creaked open *(sound)* and we stepped carefully inside. Our flashlights led us round tall ground-floor rooms, dark because of the tightly-closed shutters, dusty and strung all over with spiders'webs, and what an icky, musty smell! The old kitchen still had its awesome iron grate, and a rusty pie-safe, and the wash-house a wringer you had to turn by hand. We tried it but it didn't work any more.

Upstairs was more scary. No ghosts, but Suzy dropped her flashlight and shreiked as something soft and hairy brushed across her cheek. "It's OK" said Granpa Thrush "It's only a bat. They eat the insects so they're welcome. But watch out for raccoons, which sometimes get in when it's cold. They have a nasty bite." We didn't find any, but we did come across an old chest. Inside, instead of the treasure I was hoping for, we found dusty old clothes and an album of faded family pictures. There they were; old great-aunts in hoop skirts and great-uncles with big beards, young and old; - posing in stiff rows for the camera, and looking very severe. But the little kids all dressed up in front of them looked neat and happy. Perhaps they were still too small to have to turn the wringer!

We were looking into the past. I wondered what they all would have thought if they'd been able to look into the future, and seen pictures of how we live to-day.

The Old Farm (Part Two)

(also told by Geordie)

After the dark, scary upstairs of that old house, it was great to get outside. There was still plenty to explore.

Granpa Thrush showed us the ice cellar. You lifted up a big wooden trap-door on the ground, and steps led you down to where they'd once stored ice blocks carved out of winter ice. The ice lasted into the summer and cooled their drinks for them when it was hot. He preferred not to enter it now so as not to disturb any chicken or gopher snakes which might be there. He liked them because they ate rats and mice.

The shed had been the old kitchen, and had a partition where slaves had once slept. It was still standing, though just barely. Granpa Thrush thought we shouldn't forget things of the past, even if we now disagreed with them. They were there to remind us to live better now, if we could. In those days they made almost everything they needed at home; clothes; bread; butter; pickles; preserves; sometimes even whiskey. So they must have been busy enough without television. The kids walked to school, a one-room building several miles away, and Granpa said he'd show us where it had been.

Before we left, Granpa pulled open the rickety closet door at the back of the outhouse, and there, looking real ugly, sat a bum, half asleep. He woke with a start and lunged at Granpa with a knife. Granpa stepped back. The sleezeball closed in on him and jabbed again. I was afraid Granpa, who didn't move all that fast any more, was going to get hurt. So I skipped quickly behind the sleezeball and conked him hard on the head with Dad's stick (*sound*). He fell on the floor and we rushed off to the Sheriff as fast as Granpa's car would go. The Sheriff said the bum was probably on drugs, and dangerous.

Granpa told Dad he could be proud of me for the way I acted.

Dad said he'd expected his stick might be used to nail a snake all right, but not a snake with two legs, - and promised me all the ice-cream I wanted.

. . . .

How Daisy Trotted to Market

(A true story - as told by Suzy)

My Greatgranny Periwinkle told me she once lived on a farm, in the days when only the fanciest farmers had trucks. And since trucks and cars were very expensive, it was a rare farmer who could afford more than one.

Greatgran's husband, Ben, was a great hunter. One day, he got an unexpected invitation to shoot white-tailed deer on a ranch some hours' drive away. He was keen to go, and not remembering that the day of the hunt was market day, immediately accepted. He would probably have accepted anyway. So Greatgran was left with dozens of eggs and lots of butter to sell without a truck to carry them to the weekly market, over a mile away: no horse-cart: and no neighbors with a vehicle to share. The butter and eggs wouldn't keep till the following week, and she needed the cash to buy groceries with.

Now you might think that Greatgran would be upset and sulk, like some people would. But she had a way of taking things as they came. I bet you'll never guess how she solved this problem.

Greatgran and Grampa Ben at their farm had a herd of pigs, which from time to time were slaughtered to provide bacon. The old couple, however had become so fond of a huge sow called Daisy that she was kept on as a pet. Pigs are very bright, and Daisy was the brightest. Big

92

as a small pony, she had once charged a nasty hoodlum who looked like making trouble for Greatgran (*sound*).

Greatgran called, "Daisy, come!" (The sow always came when she was called.) Greatgran gathered her wares for market in baskets on each arm and hopped sideways on to Daisy's broad back. "Come on, now Daisy," she cried, "Get trotting!" Daisy, who never had a rider before, looked back questioningly; but with further urging started to trot, gathered speed, and before long they reached market (*sound*). People ran up to see the strange sight of sow and rider, and Greatgran could have doubled her prices. Offers to buy Daisy herself were all of course refused.

They both enjoyed the ride back (*sound*) and Ben, who was expecting to be scolded for leaving Greatgran without transportation, was amazed when he returned and learned the story. But he hard a hard time living down his a reputation as the cruel farmer who made his wife ride a pig

to market!

....

Telephone Tales – Part II – 2

A mostly true story about a

Racoon called Rambo

Suzy's cousin, Debbie, was visiting from England. She'd seen pictures of Davy Crockett and asked where the striped, bushy tail on his fur cap came from. "From a racoon" replied Suzy. "It's a cute, bow-legged animal the size of a 35 pound dog. It lives in trees, hunts for food at night, and has a nasty bite if upset. There were more common in Davy Crockett's day, but we still have some around, even in this subdivision. In fact, listen to what

happened to my fat friend Tabitha."

"Tabitha's house has a deck surrounded by a wooden

fence under some trees. One evening she noticed a small,

brown, hairy hand hanging from the top of the fence. She

was scared and called her Dad who looked and told her the

hand did look human but it belonged to a racoon asleep on

the ledge behind the fence. It would soon wake up and go

hunting for food. Now Tabitha loves eating, more than

anything, - that's why she's so fat. She felt sorry for that

poor animal having to hunt for his dinner while all she had

to do was to open the refrigerator. She thought 'Why don't

I save that racoon a lot of trouble and give it food myself?'

So she raided the kitchen and put meat and scraps by the

sleeping racoon. They were gone by the time she'd finished

her homework. The next day she put more food out for the

racoon, (she named him Rambo,) - and the day after, too. She didn't tell anyone in case they stopped her.

It was fall, getting cold, and time for blankets at night. After her usual big supper, Tabitha soon got to sleep and was dreaming of yet another plateful of brownies when, - with an almighty crash, - a horribly heavy weight slammed into her tummy - bam! (*sound*) - If she and her bed hadn't been so soft, she might have been squashed flat. She screamed and tried to throw off the heavy shape that was writhing around on top of her, grunting (*sound*); then she hollered again as teeth bit into her leg (*sound*).

Dad now rushed in to see what all the noise was about, shouted "Mom, open the front door," grabbed the beast, ran down the hall and, after getting bitten himself, heaved it onto the lawn. You've guessed! It was Tabitha's pal, Rambo the racoon. He'd got so fond of his evening meal and his friendly hostess that he'd decided to use a space in the eaves to get into the nice warm attic above Tabitha's bedroom. That was OK until he fell through the ceiling right on to Tabitha.

Moral; don't feed racoons from your home. They'll come to expect it and can turn nasty if anything goes wrong. They'll also tell their friends and they'll all want feeding!

Cousin Debbie said she'd think twice before donning a coonskin cap, even if Rambo offered her his own tail to wear.

....

An Unexpected Visitor

Geordie and little Suzy got back from school before

Mom and Dad had returned from downtown. Their teachers

had been on at them about their homework so, for once,

they decided to get down to it straightaway. They had their

heads bent over their books and were starting to write when

the doorbell rang (*sound*). Geordie went to the door and,

looking through the peephole, saw a tall, leathery, lantern-

jawed man waiting. They'd been told not to open to

strangers, so Geordie called "Who is it?". "It's cousin Dinkum from Aus-treye-lia" was the loud reply.

Geordie didn't know of any Australian cousins and though the man looked nice, even if he was leathery, Geordie didn't want him to know Mom and Dad were out. So he said "Dad'll be here soon. Please wait." "That's OK, digger" shouted the stranger through the door. "Next time, I'll tell you about Rum Jungle, where the kangaroos jump over your roof, and the crocodiles are twice as long as a Texas alligator. And about the wombats and the dingos and the ten-foot worms and the cockatoos and the koala bears and the duck-billed platypus, and about those aborigines who still believe in magic, and the world's woolliest sheep. Maybe you'd like me to bring you specimens next time. For now, it's just got to be 'G'deye'. Can't stay or I'll miss my plane".

Suzie finally got through on the phone to Dad's office, and tried to explain about the visitor. "Dad, there's a man at the door who says he's cousin Dinkum from Rum Jungle. He wants to bring us a ten-foot worm next time. For now, he just wants to say 'G'deye.' He's got to catch a plane."

"Quickly bring him inside, and keep him happy if you can till I get back" said Dad. He's a big farmer with thousands of sheep and we've business to discuss. He turns up unexpectedly when he gets bored. He brags worse than a Texan, but he's a neat guy. So give him some coffee and if I'm not back when he goes, tell him I'll call or fax."

By the time Suzy had got back to the door, the visitor had gone. He'd left a bottle of fine Australian wine on the steps and a bunch of flowers for Mom. The kids felt sorry they hadn't let him in but Dad when he got back said "Dont worry, guys, you did the right thing, - not opening to a stranger. We'll invite him stay with us on his next trip and

he'll show us pictures of those way-out beasts they have in

his part of Australia. Maybe some day he'll invite you over

there." Geordie and Suzy couldn't wait, especially at the

prospect of seeing ten-foot worms.

....

Sizzler Sockit

Sizzler Sockit was young Molly's favorite pop-star. She didn't much like his band, the Ptomaine Lobsters, but Sizzler himself was gorgeous; especially when he wore his glitzy sequin-studded outfit that flashed and shimmered as he cavorted to the music. No matter he was leathery and middle-aged and sang as if his nose was clamped tight. Molly thought his tunes exciting and she didn't at all mind him endlessly repeating the two or three words which was all they usually had - like *"Gotta go'ta, go'ta, get'ya, Baby"*.

Molly got so fond of those tunes that she kept on trying to imitate Sizzler's gravelly, rasping voice at home (*sound*), and couldn't concentrate on her school work. Her Dad asked "What's happened to your throat, honey, and why are you so mad when you sing?" — "If only I could sound half as terrific as Sizzler Sockit, I'd already be famous" she replied. "How d'you like this one:?" *'Lurve ya, lurve me, lurve ya, Baby'* she growled as angrily as she could (*sound*). —"I think you should stop practising your solos for now," said Dad, "Call me when your homework's done and maybe I'll have a surprise for you."

Dad's prescription worked wonders. Imagine her delight when he offered her two tickets for Sizzler's next concert! "You're still a bit young to go to a thing like that but this gig's supposed to be specially for pre-teens, so why don't you ask young Geordie's Mom next door if he'd like

to go with you?" Molly was beyond herself. She only

hoped Sizzler wouldn't get busted again for something and

be prevented from appearing.

Geordie didn't much like Sizzler's kind of rock. In

fact, he thought Sizzler rather a creep. But he liked Molly,

and wanted to see she'd be OK.

The concert was packed. Thousands of excited kids

thronged the auditorium. After the warm-up groups, -

Urban Lunchmeat and Nicotine Phitts, - Sizzler himself

strutted onstage, all glitz and flash. Molly and most of the

girls in the audience yelled and screamed for joy, especially

when the group struck up, *"Gotter see ya, see ya, see ya*

Babe". Even Geordie cheered a bit. Then, Sizzler started

tossing cassettes into the audience, and Geordie nailed one

as it flew past.

But, sad to say, Sizzler got involved in some toxic waste scam, and his ratings slumped. Molly, too, lost her taste for Sizzler and increasingly preferred the Country and Western songs of Ima Duck (*polka sound*) - *'Packin' it in - fer Kalamazoo -Beecause ye orr so crool*

-Leavin' it ahll - fer ever an' ever - a-rahdin a-mah ol' miule'-

....

Geordie's School Project

Geordie was assigned a school project. It was to tape

a 2 minute talk about a favorite animal and see how much

he could interest his class in it. He decided on a creature his

classmates knew of but probably weren't familiar with, and

he worked hard for several evenings. He got Dad's fine

boombox to record his talk, which would be a commentary

on the live demonstration he would be giving. The evening

before, he wandered around the yard of his home until he

found the creature he was after, and put it into a clear plastic box.

Dad, returning from a business trip, found he'd been scheduled to adress two important meetings on his new marketing plan in different places at the same time. "No problem" he said, "I'll ask my boss to pinch-hit for me at the biggest one. He doesn't know my plan but I'll give him slides to show and a detailed text I'll record for him, so he should have no trouble, however ornery his audience".

Immediately after his meeting, Dad called his boss to learn how his presentation had gone. The boss wasn't quite as warm as Dad had hoped. "I told the shareholders you'd put together a great new marketing plan. Your Secretary had mislaid the slides, but I told them they'd hear all about the plan in your very own words. When she switched on the machine to play your recording, a high clear voice explained;"

108

"Some species are permanently aquatic, with fully webbed toes. Eastern bullfrogs grow to eight inches from snout to vent. The curious horned frog of the Solomon Islands has teeth in the lower jaw in both sexes. Other Asian species have enormous webbed feet and make aerial nests between leaves overhanging water". "The audience were fascinated and wondered whether the Firm was now moving to Asia. I myself was less amused. What the deuce were you on about with those dumb frogs?"

Dad realised that someone had mixed up the tapes and he had a shrewd idea who the culprit was. Geordie got a severe dressing down and was grounded for a week. He got his frog tape back, though, and played it during his project the next day. The class were enthusiastic, especially when he demonstrated how far his common yard frog could jump when he held a housefly for him to catch. In fact, the teacher, Miss Scratchit, had trouble preventing the class

then and there from trying to jump as far as Geordie's frog.

....

Ma Soup and her Family

Two of the girls in Suzy's geography class were real chatterboxes (*sound*). Even Miss Scratchit, who usually kept her students on a pretty tight rein, hadn't been able to keep them quiet that day. So, much of the priceless information Miss Scratchit was offering her class didn't get past the chatterboxes as far as the back of the room where Suzy sat. But what she did hear really grabbed her. It was about a strange Australian lady with funny habits and a very odd family.

Suzy had heard her own folks speak about their Australian cousin Dinkum but never about this lady. So when Dad asked at dinner what Miss Scratchit had talked about at school that day, she told them. There was this fat, jolly Australian lady, Suzy explained, who served her family so much soup that people came to call her 'Ma Soup. She put her kids in fur pouches. And eventually her kids grew up and split up into women bats and bandy-legged coots. Some of them, especially the 'daisy hairs', came to no good and became known as Tasmanian devils.

At this point, Dad chimed in and said Miss Scratchit had been fairly close, but not bang on. She'd been speaking not about a lady but about a big animal family - kangaroos and others - that normally didn't much go for soup. The 'wombat' was a sort of anteater and the 'bandicoot' a kind of rabbit. The 'Tasmanian devil' was a bear-like, badger-sized beast that burrowed. They were all called 'marsupial', after a Latin word for pouch. This was because their mothers' bodies had cosy fur pockets in front, where their young felt snug and at home until they were old enough to go out and face the world. "We have a marsupial in America, too" he added; "The 'possum."

Suzy had to admit that the chatterboxes in her class might have made her miss some of Miss Scratchit's story. But in a way she was rather sorry Dad had set things straight. She would much have preferred to go on thinking about Ma Soup and her interesting family of women bats, bandy-legged coots, daisy hairs and Tasmanian devils. She decided she'd like do produce her own version of what each of them looked like, even before the next drawing class.

Would you like to be Suzy for a bit and try drawing some of her Ma Soup's family members, and perhaps tell me what kind of sound you think they make?

. . . .

Moggins

(Told by young Geordie)

Kitty Moggins, Aunt Crotchety's cat, is no ordinary
pet. In some ways, she's more like a dog. She likes to go
for short walks with one of us members of the family, and,
whenever she can, to ride in Dad's car. She'll even ride in
the basket on Aunt Crotchety's bike, though I suspect she
finds that sort of drive far too slow. She flicks her tail back

and forth in the basket, as if telling her mistress "Come on

now, lady, this isn't a funeral".

What makes Moggins extra-special is that she can't

stand milk. Imagine a cat not wanting free milk! Well,

Moggins prefers water. She's even been known to taste

some of the strong beer Aunt Crotchety's so fond of, but

Moggins knows it's powerful stuff and is content with a sip

or two. She'd hate to lose her dignity drinking too much

and not be allowed to go for any more car drives with Dad.

When a guest or baby-sitter, unaware of her tastes, happens

to offer her milk, she'll go and miaow (*sound*) at dog

Molecule, my pet. He knows what she's saying and she's

very content to watch him lap up all her milk (*sound*).

If you're not by now convinced that Moggins is a

special animal, then listen to this! One night only last

month, when Mom and Dad and were away with Molecule,

Suzy and I were asleep in our rooms. Aunt Crotchety tells

116

how she dreamed something was pulling her out of bed.

She woke up slowly and it was Moggins tugging away at

her nightdress. She could now hear a faint noise at the rear

of the house.

So she nervously got out Dad's big shotgun, hoping

to discourage any intruder who threatened, and tip-toed

after Moggins towards the back door. She pulled the

curtain back just a tad, and sure enough, she saw something

out there. It wasn't a burglar, but two big raccoons pushing

at a garbage pail in the yard. Moggins, satisfied she'd done

her duty, was by now asleep again in her basket. Aunt

Crotchety, following her example and quite relieved she

hadn't met a nasty burglar in the hall, climbed proudly

back upstairs to bed. It was only when she was putting the

shotgun back that she realised it wouldn't have been much

good as she'd forgotten to load it.

Realising how clever Moggins had been to raise the alarm, we wondered how best to reward her. In the end, we all decided she deserved the biggest bottle of the priciest mineral water we could find, as refreshment when she next went for a ride in Dad's car.

....

The Two Bit Quarter - Narrated by Himself

(Part One)

I'm quite pretty to look at, round and shiny; with a
fine face in front, a splendid eagle behind, and a fine milled
edge that's good to grasp. The 25 cents I'm worth doesn't
buy much these days, but that doesn't have to mean I don't
go far. Young Gregory Catchpole hadn't done his
homework so his Dad gave him only a quarter - me - for
pocket money one week. Gregory was so furious that he

tossed me on to the sidewalk in disgust. "A rotten old quarter? Where can I go with that?" Was he right? I'll let you judge.

Poor Old Gertrude, a handicapped lady, came hobbling along and spotted me. She bent down painfully (*sound*); - at least she thought me worth picking up - and tucked me into her shabby old purse. It already contained two sticky coughdrops, a dime and a chunk of cheese. So I was quite glad when she pulled me out with her food stamps at the grocery counter, and 'clang 'I went, into the cash register (*sound*).

I was hardly settled with my fellow coins when a horrid, raspy voice grated above me "This is a hold-up, lady. Empty that cash register into this bag, NOW, or you'll be sorry!" The next thing I knew, - the bagful of money, with me in it, was being tossed around in the hood's car as it screeched along, twisting and turning, at breakneck speed (*sound*). Before long, I heard the wailing of a siren - louder and louder-(*sound*) as the cops chased us; then - an almighty crash (*sound*) as the hood's car smashed into a tree, and our bagful of money, with me, scattered all over the road.

Now you have to feel sorry for people that get hurt in car crashes, but one advantage of being a coin is that you don't have to worry about yourself. I just bounced, rolled a little way and came to rest by the curb.

I was barely awake next morning when I heard a big road-cleaning truck grinding along. Before long, some prickly brushes whirling round spun me up and into a big metal container with all sorts of rubbish. I tried to call attention by ringing "Clang" as I hit the side, but no-one minded. The cleaning truck was quite near its dumping ground and very soon was ejecting its trash. But I was caught in a rim of the truck's scoop and lay there, glittering happily, until a lot of water suddenly hosed me away onto a

concrete floor (*sound*).

More about 'Two Bits' in Part II of this story.

Telephone Tales – Part II – 9

The Two Bit Quarter - Narrated by Himself

(Part Two)

The waste truck plant manager, whose name-label read 'MacTavish', came by inspecting. "Aha!" he cried, as he pounced on me. "Many a mickle makes a muckle!". From the funny way he spoke, he clearly came from Scotland and, I have since been told, what he meant was that if you gather enough quarters, one day you'll be rich.

The following day, we drove off very early, and by and by I heard the sound of aeroplanes (*sound*). I was a bit nervous about flying and so I think was Mr Mactavish, because it was awfully hot in his pocket. But we eventually landed safely and Mr MacTavish and I rushed off to his hotel where he changed into a kilt - (never call it a 'skirt' in front of a Scotsman, he'll be furious) - which he had to wear for a big Scottish meeting outside the city. Well, the taxi broke down. The driver didn't have a cellular phone; and no-one wanted to stop for us. No pay-phones to be seen anywhere. It was getting late and Mr Mactavish was afraid he was going to be late for his important meeting. We walked and walked and finally came to a deserted country diner, but the pretty girl behind the counter thought Mr Mactavish in his kilt looked so suspicous, she wouldn't let us in.

Only when he'd held me up and made desperate telephoning signs through the window did she open the door.

Mr Mactavish was so relieved at being able to telephone that he gave me a big kiss before dropping me into the machine (*both sounds*). It's not often coins get kissed without being washed first. Most folk are afraid, and rightly, they might pick up something nasty. To be frank, I would have preferred to have received the kiss from the pretty girl behind the counter; but it was anyway nice to feel so appreciated. And surely I could now look forward to a long and restful time before someone came to empty the payphone till.

Had it really been only two days since Gregory's Dad had given me him for pocket money? If my life goes on like this, I thought, someone might one day want to write a true story out of it. But would a reader ever believe a

humble Two Bit Quarter could have such adventures?

If you'd like to hear why I'm called 'Two-Bit', I'll

tell you in another telephone tale soon.

....

Telephone Tales – Part II – 10

Why 'Two Bit' Quarter?

Some people don't think being called 'Two Bit' is very flattering. But I'm very proud to have such an interesting name. I consider it much nicer than, say, 'Jack the Ripper' or 'Lazy Susan'. And I've heard lots of guys branded with the nickname 'Stinky', and worse. My name comes straight out of our American history, from the days of Paul Revere's gallop through the night, or Betsy Ross's stitching our first national flag.

In the days when our ancestors were often at war with the big Spanish Empire to the south, lovely gold and silver Spanish coins, some plundered, some traded, frequently found their way into our American colonies. Some were called 'dubloons', or 'pieces of eight' because they were made so as to be easily breakable into eight pieces. I'm sure you've heard the story of Treasure Island and Long John Silver, (*sing '-Yo ho ho and a bottle of rum'* *etc.,*). He as you remember considered pieces of eight well worth a sword fight and sailing across the world for, and so did lots of other sensible people.

When, after Independence, we called our new national currency the 'dollar', naming it after the German coin 'thaler'(*sound*), we still liked the old Spanish 'piece of eight'. Only instead of making our own new dollar of 100 cents actually breakable into eight pieces or bits, we just pretended it was breakable and called each eighth part, 12 +1/2 cents, - a 'bit'.

So two bits added up to 25 cents. And, early on, 'two bits', or one quarter of what used always to be a silver dollar, could buy all sorts of useful things - like a spade or even a lamb or a small pig.

So, ever since those days, our pretty and friendly 'two bit' coin has been not only an American favorite but a collectible popular abroad too. I still think that, although I'm not made of pure silver any more, I look, and feel, pretty cool compared with some of the coins you might find in peoples' pockets or purses in many countries overseas. I hope our rulers in their great wisdom think so too and will go on minting me just as I am now,- even if nowadays you need two of me to buy a soda!!

. . . .

Cats - Geordie Explains

"You can't expect cats to be all the same" Geordie

pointed out to little sister Suzy. "They nearly all like to

look down on us humans and they don't always come and

say thank-you if you help them. Of course they all like fish,

and if you threaten them can give you a terrible scratch.

They can all sometimes make a horrible racket outside in

the middle of the night (*sound*). But, like people, they come in many shapes and colors; they don't all act the same but they're still mostly cool when you get to know them."

"Let's go meet some and you'll see what I mean!" First, they said 'Hello' to Moggins, Aunt Crotchety's pitch-black cat, who likes to sleep curled up in her basket all day if she can. She only half-opened one eye to them. It might have been a wink. Then they strolled past Granpa Thrush's house. Topsitoes, his fluffy, white Tabby with blue eyes and a pretty face, lay outside inspecting the passers-by. Topsitoes, like other ladies I can think of," confided Geordie, "is picky about whom she lets touch her, but appreciates a nice compliment. So let's tell her 'Hi there, pretty kitty'. Topsitoes replied with a quick flick of her elegant tail.

Before long, they passed the little house where Poor Old Gertrude, the handicapped lady, lives. Her great protector and pet, Big Brute, sat on her front steps. (If you remember Bluto, the nasty bully in the Pop-Eye cartoons, you'll know how Big Brute looked - a battle-scarred bruiser. He also had a pointed tooth sticking out and a flattened ear).

"Big Brute looks meaner than he acts. In fact he usually enjoys a gentle caress" said Geordie as he quietly patted Big-Brute. Big Brute responded with a purr so loud it was like distant thunder (*sound*).

Meanwhile, Percival, a neighbor's cat, smart and dapper in his bright tortoise-shell coat, was clearly in a hurry to keep a date. He just gave them a quick nod as he pranced past on the other side of the street.

"People who live just for eating and never do anything are called gluttons and sloths. I'm sure Greatgranny Periwinkle was never one of those people, (she's busy as a bee and hardly eats anything), but her cat is something else; a huge, sleek, silky, calico monster who dotes on being stroked and never stops guzzling. Her name? You've probably guessed; 'Fat Cat.' As long as Fat Cat's feels she's loved and keeps on eating, she's happy." Fat Cat stretched out upside down asking for a caress as they passed, and she purred contentedly as they tickled her tummy (*sound*).

"See, Suzy, isn't it fun how cats differ, just as people do?"

. . . .

Gwendoline's Adventure

(Told by dog Molecule)

My good friend and next-door neighbor is poodle-dog Gwendoline. Her papers say she's pure- bred, but I don't need them to know she's tops as well as pricey. She's not only a fine figure of a poodle. Some claim she's even sharper than me. That's got to be doubtful but I do admit she always knows where the best bones are buried. It was a terrible shock last month when she vanished.

134

This flashy peddler had come round selling perfume. He said his scents were only for attractive people and sweet-talked Aunt Crotchety into opening the door. She allowed him to dab samples on her hand (*Sniff' sound*). Now I consider myself a super judge of all kinds of scent,- you must know we dogs can smell things much better than you people - and I thought his stuff was awful. But Aunt Crotchety seemed to like his toothy smile and bought a bottle. Frankly, I thought it smelled like garbage (*sound*).

Next day, signs were up along the street. "Poodle Missing. Reward Etc" Friend Gwendoline was gone! Neighbors- police - City Hall - gypsies - pet shops - pawnbrokers - the SPCA - the Boy Scouts - the Goodwill - a travelling circus; all were approached. None of them could help.

I was ready to bet that salesman had something to do with Gwendoline's disappearance. But how to find him?

135

Then I had an idea. I fetched something from upstairs and watched the sidewalk.

I was hoping our neighbor, Police Chief Trumpet, might pass. That evening, I did spot him driving from work. I raced after him, caught up with him as he was going into his house, and dropped what I had got from upstairs on his front steps (*crashing sound*). It was Aunt Crotchety's new perfume and the horrible scent spread all over. Captain Trumpet was furious. Of course he knew me and at once came over to complain.

Aunt Crotchety was wondering why he smelled so bad, and they were both upset with me at first. Then she recognized her perfume and told him about the salesman. Captain Trumpet began to ask questions and said he'd some checking up to do. Before long, it came out that Mr Flashy had once been involved in some illegal pet deal. The police tracked him down from the bottle label and, sure enough, found Gwendoline in his garage, awaiting Heaven knows what fate.

It was reward enough for me to have Gwendoline back none the worse from her dog-napping ordeal. But I was a bit puzzled that it was Aunt Crotchety who got all the thanks for nailing Flashy.

....

Tornado Moggins

Geordie and Suzy were looking forward to their Labor Day week-end at Uncle Pickle's ranch. Josh the foreman had fixed up horse-back riding and they were to have a monster picnic. Aunt Crotchety was going, too, but as she was scared of horses, she expected to spend a quiet day at the ranch with Moggins her cat, who was also invited.

As the week-end approached, the weather forecasts grew gloomy. A tropical storm in the Caribbean looked like veering their way. Mom and Dad decided to stick to their plans, however, and started to get the station waggon ready. It wasn't all that far, and they'd of course often been at the ranch. But you know how it is with a family trip. The car gradually fills up with food, clothes, boots, kites, tennis rackets, picnic gear, bags, boxes, dog Molecule's bowl (yes, he was going too), and all sorts of paraphenalia. It's a miracle, once it's all loaded, that driver and passengers fit in as well.

Still, in spite of pit stops for Suzy and dog Molecule, they made good time. But the weather grew worse and they arrived with the rain pelting down and the wind howling (*sound*). It was worse next morning and, clearly, there wasn't going to be any horse-back riding or picnic. So the kids got down to dominos, - at which Geordie was a dab-

139

hand, and a long-jump contest in the barn, - which dog Molecule won easily. Aunt Crotchety said she'd show them how to long-jump another time as she had to watch Batman on Channel 3.

Kitty Mogins liked television too. But she must have missed the flashing tornado warnings urging people to stay indoors, because after lunch she slipped out, unseen, on some urgent errand.

The family kept warm inside, listening to the furious storm. Once during the afternoon, a sound like a freight train nearly deafened them (*sound*) - followed by a terrible crash (*sound*) and even worse torrential rain (*sound*). Only then they realised Moggins was nowhere to be seen. As soon as things got quieter, they sallied out in search of her, sloshing around (*sound*) in the ankle-deep water left by the storm. One shed and a pig-trough were gone, but no other big damage. They searched and called (*sound*). Nothing.

Now they were worried, and more so the next morning when she was still gone. "Poor, poor Moggins!" sobbed Aunt Crotchety. "Perhaps she slunk out because I forgot her mineral water." (Moggins didn't like milk).

Everyone was still sadly searching when dog Molecule started barking by the water tower (*sound*). Drawing nearer, they heard a faint squeak (*sound*), looked up, and there on the water tower where the tornado had swept her up, wet-through and shivery, crouched Moggins, clinging to the wreck of the pig-trough. Quickly they fetched her down, rubbed her hard, gave her some nice hot water to drink and put her next to the stove. Before long she started to purr and snooze, and next day, back home, she was snug in her basket again and, should I say (?), 'right as rain'?

. . . .

The Gypsy's Prediction

Geordie was riding his bike one evening near his home when a shabby old station waggon slowly passed him. It was full of children and dogs, and a lot of junk. The kids and the dogs were bawling at each other (*Sound*). The driver was a dark, elderly lady wearing several necklaces and huge silver earrings. Geordie thought he recognized a gypsy family his Dad had noticed when they had visited the carnival. What he also saw was that one of the car's tires was very low; low enough for a policeman in a bad mood to give the driver a ticket for driving a dangerous vehicle.

Geordie pedalled hard and caught up with the jaloppy. He tapped on the window and pointed to the tire. The car creaked to a halt (*sound*) and the lady yelled at the kids inside to be quiet (*sound*). She explained to Geordie her tire valve had gone and she didn't have a spare. She was winging it back to her mobile home, hoping the tire would hold out and that she didn't pass a cop.

Geordie had been told not to get involved with strangers and didn't think his Dad would like his car tools to be used in a situation of this kind. But he felt sorry for the gypsy lady and thought he might do her a good turn. He'd only recently helped his Dad blow up a leaking tire and temporarily fix it with a special adhesive, and he knew where that was kept.

Telling the lady to hang in for a few minutes, he hurried back to fetch Dad's pump and adhesive. He could hear her shouting at her kids to be quiet all the way to his house, and they didn't stop screaming until he returned with his equipment. He had trouble pumping up such a heavy car (*sound*) - but he managed, and quickly applied the adhesive.

Then he shouted "Go lady… I don't know how long it'll hold, so step on it!" The kids were yelling again but Geordie just heard the lady's prediction as she pulled away "Thank you, young lad. I see you going far in life!"

As Geordie had expected, his Dad was doubtful about Geordie's accosting the gypsy lady, even if it was to do her a good turn. But he commended him for his kind thought and added "Normally I don't believe in fortune-tellers, but the station waggon lady may coincidentally have got something right when she thanked you. She said she saw you 'going far'. Well, I just got a letter from your Scottish cousins inviting Suzie and you to spend part of your next vacation with them. And no-one could say Scotland isn't far off!"

....

Telephone Tales – Part II – 15

'Scots Wha Hae'

Geordie and Suzy were to spend the summer in

Scotland. They were excited at the prospect, but it would

be their first time away from home and they had mixed

feelings. Mom and Dad were flying over with them but it

was a real wrench to hug dog Molecule and kitty Moggins, -

and even Aunt Crotchety,- goodbye for a whole month.

Next to Suzy in the aeroplane sat a bewhiskered Scot.

He was too busy enjoying his whisky to say much during

146

the long flight, but as they were leaving he grasped her shoulders, looked at her earnestly, and said "You're a lucky wee lassie to be going to Britain. But never forget 'Scots wha hae wi' Wallace bled'." Suzy knew a cat called Wallace but didn't think her neighbor meant him so she decided to ask her cousins Lennox and Fiona who Wallace was.

The cousins lived in a big stone house on the edge of a little village. A warm lunch of broth, pasties and salmon, with tasty oat cakes, helped reduce the kids' jet lag. Fiona gave them woolly underwear and lovely Scots tartan mufflers in case they found the summer too cold, and Lennox took them out for their first drive in the country. Geordie marvelled at the lots of ancient castles, some in ruins, some still lived in; and reflected (rightly) that the people then must have been at least as fond of fighting each other as the cowboys and Indians had been back home.

Lennox explained that the Wallace mentioned by the old Scot on the 'plane was a great Scots hero who long ago had beaten the English in battle.

Suzy liked the thousands of sheep on the green hillsides and, once, they spotted a big red deer, with enormous antlers, high up in the forest.

In the weeks that followed, the kids got to see lots of things new to them; like the massed bands of pipers parading in front of majestic, floodlit, Edinburgh castle. They attended a 'ceidligh' (pronounced 'kayly') - a party with one lively Scottish square dance after another. Cousin Lennox, old though he was, quite tired them out showing them steps for the reel. Geordie picked up some new words - such as 'Hoots mon!'(meaning 'shucks!'), - 'wisht!' ('be quiet!') - and 'I'm away to ('now leaving for') lunch'- which he thought he'd try out on Miss Scratchit, his teacher, when they got back to the States.

A lot of rain fell, but nothing stopped for it, not even

a day of Highland games where they saw the caber, a log

big as a tree, being tossed, and a monster hammer thrown.

Most of all they liked Scottish shortbread and hoped it had

been available long ago to help console people when they

were fighting all those dreadful battles.

They were having a great time but were missing

Mom and Dad and dog Molecule and even Aunt Crotchety,

and at the end of their letter home they added "'Love' and

'Wisht!' from Geordie, 'Hoots, Mon!' from Suzie, and

'Scots wha hae!' from us both".

. . . .

'Cifer' and Company

(told by Geordie)

I'm not too fond of my classmate Zoltan but my Dad knows his Dad. So, when Suzy and I got invited to his home the other day, we went. Zoltan was on his best behavior but what surprised us more was the number of cats in his house. I counted four. They were all different but, even so, how to remember their names? Zoltan's Mom heard my question.

"They're called 'Alog' (pronounced like 'a log'),

'Spaw', 'Swhiskers', and 'Cifer' (pronounced 'See fer')"

she said. We had to ask "Why on earth did you choose such

funny names and how d'you know which is which? ". "It's

not so difficult" replied Zoltan's Mom. First comes 'Alog'.

He has the darkest coat and his name starts with letter 'A'.

'Spaw's a lot lighter in color and his initial 'S' is later in the

alphabet, so he gets to be next. 'Swhiskers' is nearly white,

so he follows. 'Cifer's coat is all sorts of colors, but we got

him after the others so he comes last.

We didn't want to be rude but she hadn't told us

everything. So we asked, politely, "But how come you hit

on those odd names?" "Many people ask that." she replied.

"They're really all normal words which have something to

do with 'cat'. You might already have guessed one or two.

'Alog' is of course short for 'catalog', which can mean a list

of anything from crimes to goodies. 'Cat's paw', meaning

somebody's stooge, doesn't sound very flattering either, but Kitty 'Spaw' thinks it's a great name, and it's short enough to be able to repeat really fast (*sound*). That's useful because she doesn't always come at the first call, even for evening milk.

'Tswhiskers' isn't so easy to repeat quickly (*demonstrate*). But what cat wouldn't like to be able to say "I'm the cat's whiskers"? All four names - 'Alog', 'Spaw', 'Tswhiskers' and 'Cifer' are quite charming once you get used to them; and, after all, every cat likes to be called something more special than 'Kitty, Kitty, Kitty'."

"But what about 'Cifer'?" we asked. (It wouldn't have done for us to come across him later on, not knowing why he was called that.) "That's the easiest of all." replied Zoltan's Mom." 'A' for apple; 'B' for bubblegum, 'C' for cat".

. . . .

The Medal Award Haircut

Mom used to be the one to cut her children's hair; but when she got a job, she had much less time so she sent Geordie and Suzy to the local hairdresser. He wasn't the best of all barbers, but his shop was at least close by. Dad had stopped getting his hair cut there because the barber was a terrible chatterbox and never stopped asking questions as his scissors went 'snip-snip-snip'-(*sound*). He seemed even nosier with Geordie and his sister; "So what do you do first when you come home from school?"

"How's your math coming along under Miss Scratchit?"

"What d'you have for breakfast?" "How many times have

you worn that dress?" "How does Mom like her new job?

Dy'all eat much broccoli at home and how does your Mom

prepare it?" and so and so on and so on. The kids didn't

encourage him by long answers, but every time he seemed

to become more and more inquisitive.

During the recent floods, Geordie had quietly rescued

a kitten from drowning in the Bayou behind his school. It

was rash of him to do it because he could have been swept

away. He thought no-one had seen him and wasn't going to

tell anybody, not knowing that the principal himself had

witnessed it all from his window. Now, he was going to be

given a bravery medal by the Mayor, no less!

He felt rightly proud of the big honor as the Mayor

bent over him and hung the medal ribbon round his neck.

But he knew the barber at his next haircut would quizz him mercilessly about every detail of the ceremony. So he decided on a new tack.

The medal-giving in the school auditorium was shown on television and written up in the newspapers. "Schoolboy hero awarded medal". But, sure enough, at the next haircut, the barber was on at him again. "So it was the Mayor himself who took time off from his busy schedule to give you that splendid award!" he gushed, as his scissors went 'Snip-snip-snip' (*sound*). I would have died from pride and joy in your place, but you looked almost bored. Of course I'd never have worn those black pants for that occasion but I suppose that was your Mom's choice, wasn't it? I noticed Miss Scratchit actually smiling in the front row. 'snip-snip-snip-(*sound*).' "But the Mayor seemed to be whispering something to you as he bent over you and draped the black ribbon round your neck. More

155

congratulations, no doubt? I'd just love to know, - or is it a secret?"

"No secret at all" replied Geordie. "What he said was - Where did you get that awful haircut?"

The Pet Alligators

Tabitha, Molly and Suzie were talking about pets one day during a class break. Tabitha was insulted because she'd looked after her cat a lot but it had just wandered off without so much as a thank-you lick. She was wondering what sort of pet to ask for next. A dog might do but Tabitha was very fat and didn't much like the thought of having to take it for a run or even a walk. Maybe something different but not too difficult to care for; a sheep, perhaps? That could help keep the grass down in their big yard. Or an Emu - an enormous Australian ostrich-like bird that she could ride on. But what did it eat and would it be happy sleeping in their garage? Molly, too, was looking for another pet. She'd already had problems with a racoon she'd fed too much. It had grown so fond of her that it invaded the loft above her bedroom and one night fell through the ceiling right on top of her. She went for exotic sorts of pet - maybe a big slow snake, or a warthog (*sound*)? But, on reflexion, she wondered whether her Mom would take to them. They weren't the sort you could just keep hidden for ever. And it would probably take ages to get the right permit.

Just then, Herbert came up. He'd heard them talking and said. "Pets? My uncle in Louisiana loved alligators so much, he kept one in his old back-yard jacuzzi. He fed it left-overs from the butcher's. It was called Aristotle and one day it chased the man who came to read the meter, but only because he shouted nasty names at it (*sound*), and threw rocks at it. My uncle said Aristotle was more useful and less expensive than a burglar alarm. Indeed, as soon as the City came and took Aristotle away, a burglar stole their TV."

Suzy surprised them all. Well, your uncle may have had an alligator. We've no less than four alligators in our back bathroom. "Go on, Suzie! You expect us to believe that?" they shouted. "You're just saying that because you haven't got any fun ideas about new pets, like we've been talking about." But Suzie didn't back off. "I bet each of you a candy bar I'm right. You come to our house next week after school and I'll show you our four alligators, all grinning and green, in our back bathroom. OK?" They rather doubtfully agreed, more because they each wanted a candy bar off Suzie than because they really believed her.

When the time came, Suzie was as good as her word, and they felt a bit scared when she took them to the back of her house. She threw open the bathroom door and there, sure enough, on the bathtub wall, vividly pictured in big ceramic tiles, were four green, grinning alligators. She said "There they are! A bit on the small side, but much more comfortable to watch while you're having your bath than having live ones with you in the tub! Now my three candy bars, please!"

. . . .

Sammy Snake

Molly liked snakes. Her friend Suzie thought they were nasty, and bit people, and didn't have any feelings except angry ones. Cats were a lot nicer and more affectionate. Molly believed snakes had a right to their privacy like anyone else and didn't want to blame them if they bit somebody who'd trodden on them or was about to. In a circus, she'd once seen an Indian snake charmer blowing into his flute made from a gourd, and charming the snake into rising up out of its basket and waving in time

with the music (*sound*). "I'd like to see your Kitty Moggins

do that!" she pointed out to Suzie. Suzie replied that

Moggins was her Aunt Crotchety's cat and Aunt Crotchety

couldn't play even on ordinary flute - let alone one made

from a gourd. If she ever did learn to do so, maybe she

could train Moggins, too, to rise up out of her basket and

wave around in time to the music (*sound*). Molly didn't

think Moggins would ever learn to like music that much,

and she hoped Suzie wasn't right about snakes having no

feelings for people.

　　She decided to ask her uncle Homer, who'd once

worked at the Zoo and had a pet python. "Well," said

Homer, "Snakes are reptiles and cold-blooded creatures and

don't relate all that easily to humans. But, like people, they

appreciate being cozy and getting enough to eat, and now

and again, when they've had a chance to really get to know

someone, they've been shown to miss them if they're separated. There was this lady who had a pet snake called Sammy.

Her job was to dance in a night club with Sammy round her neck (*sound*). One day she had to go North and leave Sammy with us at the Zoo. After a while, Sammy went off his food. He wouldn't touch even the fattest rat. As he was getting very thin, we telephoned the lady." "I'll send you a hanky scented with my perfume." She said. "It will remind Sammy of me and it may make him feel better and eat again."

"The hanky was placed in Sammy's cage. Now a snake doesn't purr to tell you when he's pleased, but Sammy did remember the scent, started chomping down everything he was given, and grew sleek and happy again." Molly was very glad to hear that snakes can remember people like that; but she decided that she wouldn't go for a pet snake herself just yet. "If I ever get a job dancing in a

night club and can find a snake as nice as Sammy, then

maybe. But for the time being, I think I'll have to make do

with my hamster."

. . . .

The Litter Lout

Geordie's and Suzy's Mom and Dad were being visited by a family from overseas. Victor, the visitors' small son, was prone to car sickness and when Mom and Dad were going to drive them round the hill country, they persuaded Aunt Crotchety to look after him. Attending an American school in his own tropical country, he had no trouble speaking English, and the grown-ups thought it would be good for all three kids to be together for a week-end.

The visiting parents were charming, but neither they nor the American school seemed to have done a lot for Victor. He didn't want to keep his things in order. He shouted rude things at Kitty Moggins (*sound*). He scattered his clothes all over the bedroom floor. He was sloppy with a knife and fork, and when kindly Suzy wanted to help him, he spilled his soup over her lap (*sound*). He tossed his ice cream dessert into the living room fire (it was beginning to get cold outside) and screamed with laughter when it all went hissing up the chimnney (*sound*). He didn't ever say 'thank you'. Most annoying of all, he took all Geordie's old toys and littered them all over the lawn. When Aunt Crotchety told him about the house rules and how he was supposed to behave, he grabbed Suzy's sweet little flaxen-haired doll and threw it to the snapping turtle in the lily pond. (*sound*)

Aunt Crotchety knew Victor was still a small guy, and in a strange country, and she didn't want to make him think Americans nasty and cruel.

She was tempted to give him the good paddling she felt he deserved but Victor, even if he was a little brute, was a house guest. However, house guests whatever their ages are supposed to behave nicely towards their hosts and not litter things all over the yard. So she told him sternly "Victor - You're a guest and I don't expect you to do exactly as we all do in this house. But one thing I have to insist on: that is, that you don't leave all sorts of things lying around outside. You won't ever catch us taking things outside and leaving them there."

It snowed heavily that night. In the morning, everything was covered, crisp and sparkling white; trees, lawn, bushes, driveway, mail-box, the street, even the street lantern. Aunt Crotchety knew Victor's country didn't have snow, and wanted to give him a pleasant surprize. "Look, Victor!" she cried expectantly, taking him outside. Victor, however, took one long look all around, then exclaimed, furiously, "Who's gone and left all this stuff lying around?"

. . . .

The Balloon Sandwich

It was Geordie's birthday and, since he'd got some really fine grades at school, Dad offered him and Suzie a ride in a hot air balloon as reward.

Dad drove them to the take-off place and they watched a huge fan slowly-inflating the enormous piece of fabric, until it finally raised itself erect in the form of a gigantic tear-drop, seven stories high. As Geordie watched the pilot light the gas burner, it suddenly shot out an eight foot flame, with a terrible roar, up into the balloon (*sound*). Geordie almost jumped out of his skin. The crew said not to worry. It was only that noisy burner producing the hot air which was to lift them way up into the sky. Everything was OK and ready for lift-off.

The huge balloon was straining away at the guy ropes and the two kids were helped into the wicker-work basket in which they were to ride. The pilot got in too. As the rising hot air from the burner above them pushed up the massive tear-drop and tautened its moorings, the pilot gave the word to 'let go', and up they soared.

It was the kids' first balloon ride and they marvelled as everything on the ground grew smaller and smaller as they rose. The ground crew soon looked like midgets, then like ants. They could see their subdivision below, the houses looking like so many matchboxes.

And just when they recognized their school and were wondering whether one of the tiny flea-like figures way down there outside it might be Aunt Crotchety or Miss Scratchit, a great damp cloud unexpectedly enveloped them and they could barely see each other through the mist.

Geordie was getting out his monster lunch sandwich, heavily laced with mayo, the way he liked it. But the pilot said they'd have to go down. It wasn't safe to continue in that cloud. In moving to adjust the burner, he accidentally knocked the sandwich from Geordie's hands, and it sailed over the edge of their basket out into the cloud, and down... down.

Meanwhile, Police Chief Trumpet on his front steps was just taking off his hat, and getting out his keys, when a heavy squashy shape burst on his bald head and trickled down his back and shirt front (*sound.*). He whipped round and, jerking out his pistol, angrily shouted "Who's there?"

But of course no-one answered. So he postponed his lunch and furiously searched the whole subdivison for the culprit. He was still searching even after Geordie and Suzie had got back home.

As it happened, Captain Trumpet was due to be having lunch with the family the very next day, and Dad thought it as well to ask Mom to be sure not to serve Geordie's favorite sloppy mayo sandwich. I wonder why.

Telephone Tales – Part II – 22

The Great Big Hole

Dad was anxious to get a letter off by the next

collection and asked Geordie to drop it by the Post Office

for him first thing next morning. Geordie thought he might

as well jog there. And as he ran past Granpa Thrush's

house on Skirmish Road, he was just admiring a pretty

sapsucker perched high on a branch when he all but

dropped into an enormous hole in the sidewalk. It was

173

deeper than his front door was high and a real menace, especially to anyone not looking where he was going.

He took a different way back and forgot about the hole until after breakfast, when someone called to say that Granpa Thrush had fallen into it and couldn't get out. Old Granpa could see quite well with his glasses but this morning he was already taking his walk when he realised he'd left them behind; and the next moment - crash! yaoucks! - and there was Granpa way down in the hole. You couldn't even see his head sticking up above the sidewalk, he was so far down.

Of course people rushed up to help. But although they tugged, gently and then more firmly (*sound*), Granpa was stuck down there below. He didn't seem to be hurt so they brought him his breakfast right there in his hole. In the end they had to bring an enormous mechanical digger to excavate under Granpa, whose foot was jammed in

174

something hard, deep down. To keep him as happy as they could, they brought him another breakfast and a beer. But it took hours before they finally managed to bring up both Granpa and the thing in which his foot had been caught. You'll never guess what it was!

Apparently the ground under the Skirmish Road sidewalk had been subsiding over a good many years, and now it had to caved in altogether. What no one had known, however, was that the Civil War encounter between Union and Confederate troops which had given the road its name had been more than a mere skirmish, since heavy cannon had been involved. And it was in the mouth of one of those cannons that Granps' foot had lodged when he fell into the hole.

Since it was he who had found the cannon, Granpa claimed it as his. When they found it was still fully loaded ready to fire, however, he made them go much more slowly with the mechanical digger in case it struck a spark that

detonated the cannon and shot it off. They re-assured

Granps that the gunpowder was probably too damp to ignite

after all those years, but Granps made them pour several

buckets of water in, to make sure. When he finally got clear

of the hole, he said it was fine having your own cannon, but

not if it was going to shoot you out of it in front of your

own front door!

Telephone Tales – Part II – 23

The Witch and the Clockabill (Part Three)

You will remember that after Sniffy the witch had turned dragon Rumbold into a clockabill, he had become rich. He now enjoyed such a comfortable life, with endless root-beer, a sleek, red, open sports car and a bunch of hip, slender, laughing maidens lolling about in his swimming pool, that Sniffy decided to turn herself into one of those maidens.

She hadn't been all that good-looking as a witch but now, as a hip, slender, laughing maiden, she looked really stunning and could have got a job advertising beauty soap any time, or so she thought as she admired herself in one of the full-length mirrors in Rumbold's cave. It was when she said 'Hi!' to one of the other maidens coming in from the swimming pool that she got a terrible shock. Her figure had changed for the better all right, but her voice was still the old scratchy, croaky voice of Sniffy the witch (*sound*). She tried again, and the girl who had come in was so scared, she ran straight back into the pool.

"I must have done the spell wrong" thought Sniffy. So she tried it again, and again, but it didn't help. Either she turned herself back into Sniffy the nasty witch, or into the slender laughing maiden with the horrible voice. So she flew off to consult her friend Moony. Moony was even uglier than Sniffy had been, but very wise. She said Sniffy

178

would have to stay as she was until she did someone a good turn. Sniffy had never done anyone a good turn before, and it took her ages before she decided she would ask Rumbold if he wanted to drop being a busy rich clockabill and go back to being a normal lazy dragon again.

Rumbold wasn't at all sure. He would certainly welcome not being woken up by alarm clocks in his head every hour. But he knew it took a lot of work to be rich and enjoy his lovely cave with its endless fountains of root beer and so on. So in his deep voice he replied "Thank you, Sniffy, -what I'd really like is to be able to change back into a normal dragon every now and again, when I need a rest from working hard, but then to become a clockabill again when I have to pay my debts. If you could fix that for me, I'd let you use my sleek red open sports car as soon as you got your driver's licence". "Done!" croaked Sniffy, happily. She now saw that by doing someone a good turn, she not only helped them, but she could be offered a

kindness in return. And how she longed to drive that car!

And will you believe that, just as Moony had said,

the moment she shook hands with Rumbold and allowed

him to change back into being a dragon when he wanted,

she went on being a hip, slender, laughing maiden and

spoke with a really groovy voice, too I.

The Witch and the Clockabill (Part Four)

Sniffy the witch, who had used her magic to transform herself into one of Dragon Rumbold's hip, slender laughing maidens, now had his permission to use his sleek red open sports car. She had been longing to drive it ever since she had laid eyes on it behind Rumbold's splendid cave.

But first she had to pass her driver's test. Now Sniffy was still a first-rate busybody. She had already criticized all the other laughing maidens' hair-dos. But she was hopeless at steering a car. On her first driving lesson she drove straight into an ice-cream van. On the second, she side-swiped a police car and forced it into the ditch. Just as well you didn't hear what the policeman said! On her third try, she ran into a lamp-post. Rumbold's car insurance was getting tired of paying the huge bills and the other maidens giggled every time she got into the car. She wondered if she'd ever pass her test.

It was only when her ugly old friend Moony reminded her of the spell for changing things into sparrows that she began to improve. Whenever she risked colliding into something, she would quickly whisper '*Nu ska du bli sparv, dumbom!*' (*sound*), and of course whatever she was going to collide into would become a sparrow,- peep *'tweep tweep* '- and fly away. So, on her fourteenth try, she finally got her driver's licence. Her only problem now was that the longer she remained a hip, slender, laughing maiden, the

harder it grew for her to cast spells. So whenever she was

driving Rumbold's splendid Ferrari alone, she'd turn herself

back into Sniff the Witch again; just to keep up her magic

skills.

One day, while driving on the Freeway, she was

absorbed in rehearsing her spells. Suddenly, the wail of a

police siren (*sound*) and flashing lights jolted her back to

earth. Unfortunately, it was the same policeman she had

once driven into the ditch. 'Lady' he snarled, as he took out

his book of tickets - 'you were doing ninety miles an hour.'

What Sniffy most of all wanted to do then was to turn him

into a toad; but she could only remember the spells for

changing him into a fairy or a sparrow, - both of them far

too good for him, she thought, and they only lasted a week.

Anyway, *'Nu ska du bli sparv, dumbom'* she hissed.

'Tweep tweep' he chirupped, - and fluttered daintily away.

'Such a pity I couldn't remember how to turn him into a toad,' reflected Sniffy as she drove on - very carefully. She'd almost got back to Rumbold's cave before she remembered to change herself back into a hip, slender, laughing maiden again. And the other maidens all wondered why an angry little sparrow kept on flying over Sniffy's head for a whole week.

Ma Bell - a story based on fact

A Japanese business friend of Dad's gave Susie a pretty silver-colored Koi. She was much more delighted with the fish than Dad was. "Where on earth will we put it?" he grumbled. "We've no bowl big enough in the house, and until I get a raise, my plans for the yard won't include a pool. But - O.K - as long as you feed it, Susie!"

In the end, Granpa Thrush lent them his glass aquarium in which he'd once kept pet lizards. It fitted nicely under the living room window near the telephone. So they called the fish 'Ma Bell'. One of Susie's other jobs was to answer the phone when her parents were out, and whenever she did so, she sprinkled some fish food on to the water. She loved seeing Ma Bell zoom to the surface, and hungrily gulp down her pellets - slurp, gulp (*sound*).

Now water transmits sound better than air, and Ma Bell, who was no dummy, quickly learned that a ringing phone meant food from Susie. In fact, if nobody answered the phone by the end of the second ring, Ma Bell surged to the surface anyway and slapped her tail on the water to get attention. The family at first thought it was amusing and pandered to her impatience by rewarding her with food. Of course, the more pellets she gulped down, the bigger she grew, and, if she wasn't immediately fed, the more water she splashed. As the carpet was getting soaked as a result of her antics, they moved the telephone to the next room.

But Ma Bell could hear it better than anyone else, and splashed even worse. After that, they disconnected the phone altogether; and missed several important calls.

You might think Ma Bell was at risk from Kitty Moggins, whose favorite food was tuna. Not on your life! One day, Moggins was taking a quiet nap on the carpet near the tank, and the phone rang (*sound*). Ma Bell got upset no-one was answering and splashed so violently that she leaped right out of the tank. Furiously twisting and thrashing about, she landed right on top of Moggins, who was terrified and raced upstairs.

Aunt Crotchety ran down and was almost as scared at the madly writhing fish as Moggins had been. She would have yelled 'Help!' but no-one else was home so, grabbing a wicker-work trash basket, she bravely scooped the monster fish off the floor and dumped her back into the water. She consoled Ma Bell by emptying the whole package of fish food into her tank, and covered it with the

big fireplace hearth-rug. Dad canceled a family trip to the

ocean next week-end; and, with the money saved, installed

a fish pond in the yard. He placed it as far as possible from

the house, not of course to protect Ma Bell from Moggins,

but to make sure she couldn't hear the telephone at all.

About the Author

Oxford Scholar and University boxing middleweight; a WWII Commando; a British diplomat, winding up as British Ambassador to El Salvador; once kept a pet javelina; father of four and granddad of (so far) six; Michael Wenner has a published autobiography and two minor books. He wrote Telephone Tales mainly to entertain his family but the stories — short and colorful enough to read successfully by phone — have proved popular with fifth and sixth grade students taught by the author as a volunteer teacher, and much further afield; hence their publication now for readers young and old.

The author lives in Houston, with Beastlet, his pet guinea-pig; and his wife, sixth generation Houstonian and former zookeeper.